THE SEARCH FOR SETH

BARTON ANDERSON
BOOK 2

GK BEATTY

Chiselbury

Published by Chiselbury Publishing, a division of Woodstock Leasor Limited

14 Devonia Road, London N1 8JH, United Kingdom

www.chiselbury.com

ISBN: 978-1-916556-36-2

1

"**C**ome on, Smoke! Don't be a baby about this!"

That was the attitude of Barton Anderson, as he tried to convince his big gray friend that traveling in the railroad cattle car would be more than adequate this day.

Barton's reasoning was that the train would cut their travel time in half and give them both a chance to rest after the long ride from Prestonburg. Also, the train offered the chance of entering Lawrence with less detection, as they would be able to disembark in the middle of town, start looking for Angus Ford's sister, and get a bearing on the location of their main objective... Seth.

Once Smoke stepped into the railroad cattle car, Barton started working his way to the passenger coach. Even though he would leave his saddle and bedroll with Smoke, to give him something familiar to relate to, Barton flung his saddlebag over his shoulder, checked his Colt sidearm, and carried the big Henry rifle under his arm. Since he entered into his current undertaking, he had learned one major truth, "You may not expect trouble, but you are always prepared for it."

There were a lot of people in town this day, and it seemed like a sizeable part of them would be going out of Smithview on this train. Lawrence was a destination for people who were looking for a larger choice for shopping, eating, entertainment, and business affairs. And, if anyone were going on to the state capital, they could catch the Topeka Flyer locomotive there, and be in the center of the government in less than an hour. Barton was planning, and hoping, that all of his affairs could be settled in Lawrence and any further travel would be returning to Smithview...him, Smoke, and Seth.

Barton enters into the last railroad coach before the cattle car. The choices of where to sit are dwindling quickly, so he moves into a seat closest to the back door. Placing his saddle bag in the seat next to him, Barton slowly lowered himself upon the unpadded seat, arraigning his long legs in a manner to be comfortable for the ninety-minute trek. Once settled in, with his Henry rifle resting between his hands, Barton figures to use the travel time to think about his plan to find Angus Ford's sister, assess the situation, get Seth out as safely as possible, and return to Smithview. He had already accepted the truth that it would not be as simple as 'taking Seth home'. A lot has changed since the last time Barton saw his youngest son, and a lot will have to be carefully explained.

Jeff, Barton's brother-in-law who was now tending to the Anderson homeplace, had offered to take Smoke back to the ranch and let him live there if anything happened to Barton. Surely, Jeff and Sally wouldn't be closed to the idea of taking in a real family member. Barton was no longer in a position to offer Seth a stable life and a home base. All he could be was a father who would love, provide, and protect his only son...from a distance. So many thoughts, options, and realities were racing through Barton's mind until a strange voice interrupted his contemplations.

"Excuse me, sir! I hate to intrude upon your time of reflection, and if I had any other options, I would gladly consider them. But your saddle bag is occupying the last seat on the train. I would gladly hold it in my lap if you would let me exchange places with it."

Just as Barton turned toward the stranger, prepared to give him one of those looks that had caused many drifters to just keep moving, the tall man notices that the stranger is an elderly man. And, if that wasn't enough to catch Barton's scrutiny, the ministerial collar that the gentleman is wearing did. Barton doesn't say a word, he just grabs his saddle bag, lifts it away from the seat, and nods his head for the cleric to prepare for the train to leave.

Upon working his aged frame into the cramped space, the soft-spoken gent sighs a breath of relief and introduces himself.

"My name is Father Lucas Porter. I am a longtime padre of various missions around the fine state of Kansas. Now, I am on my way to Lawrence to be retired to a final life chapter of providing love and leadership to precious souls at the orphanage there. You could say that I have been taking care of God's children my whole life, no matter what age they may be."

Barton continues looking out the window of the railroad coach, hoping that the next ninety minutes are not going to be a gabfest with his coincidental traveling companion. Maybe he should have just ridden Smoke to Lawrence, at least there was a better chance of solitude on the open road. The old minister places his humble travel bag on the floor, between his feet, leans his head forward, and closes his eyes. Barton hoped that maybe this was a sign that the old man would be sleeping, or praying, for the rest of the trip. He even thought of praying for such a thing, but Barton still had a hard time talking with the Almighty about anything.

As the wheels of the train sing out a rhythmic chatter over the rails, and the railcar sways between the guiding ribbons of steel, Barton settles back into the prospects of the future with Seth in his life, and his keeping up the expectations that the state had for him as 'the Janitor'. There was one thing that Barton knew for sure, and that was that the wrong people could never make a connection between him and a surviving family member. Even with a heart that had grown cold with hate, rage, and revenge, the gripping thought of reliving the loss of family sent a shiver up his spine. He was prepared to do whatever it took to make sure that Seth had a full life, including riding off and never seeing his youngest child again.

The more he thought about it, the option of Jeff and Sally raising Seth was becoming the best option to take. They loved it when Seth and Adam would visit, their kids treated his boys like they were their siblings, and the addition of one more would not be an intimidating consideration. Barton would continue to put a large part of his compensation money, that he got from his successful removal of murderous outlaws, in the special Smithview bank account he had set up for Jeff and Sally. While it was initially purposed to help with the running of the ranch, Barton was confident there would be enough there to put food in another mouth, clothes on another back, and shoes on another pair of feet. Barton would continue to keep his distance from the ranch itself, not allowing anyone to make any quick links between him and any particular member of the family living there. Maybe, from time to time, Barton could get a signal to Seth to meet him at Rooster Pass, especially that special place where Barton used to take the boys to fish and Jenny for a picnic. Jason Nash, Reverend Sutton, and Marshal Tomes could be trusted to help communicate messages between the tall man and the family on the ranch. As this, increasingly, seemed to be a workable plan, Barton starts to settle into his seat and close his eyes for some rest before arriving in Lawrence. At least, that was his plan until...

"Sir, I can't help but notice that you seem to have a lot on your mind. The way you place your hands around that Henry rifle, and squeeze, can divulge a lot to a person, if that person takes the time to notice," the old priest shares, without really being provoked by Barton or anyone.

Barton continues to keep his eyes closed, facing away from the chattery churchman, hoping that maybe the lack of response would be taken as a clear sign that he wasn't interested in any new conversations, new friends, or new advice from anyone, this day or anytime soon.

Father Porter, sensing that his vocational gifts may be needed by the man sitting next to him, continues, "That's the problem with the world, people are too busy to take the time to notice that they are surrounded by afflicted folks who are communicating loudly to them, and yet not saying a single word verbally. I am getting that feeling with you, Mr. Anderson."

With that unexpected proclamation, Barton opens his eyes, turns his head toward the old clergy, and waits for the next words to come, and the next shoe to drop, before he reacts to where this moment is going to take them.

"Yes, I know who you are. I have known from the time I got on the train. I knew when I asked if I could sit by you. You see, with all the people rustling around, I could have missed your lofty stature and the make of that rifle in your hands. But I noticed you when you were having difficulty getting the contrary gray horse to join you on this train. Sir, I was born at night, but not last night, and I added things up fairly quickly."

Barton, turning his head away and looking out the window,

responds, "I guess you probably wish there had been a few more open seats available, so you wouldn't have to sit with someone like me, padre?"

The old priest smiles, runs his fingers through his thinning, white hair, and answers, "If I had a problem sitting next to you, and there was no other place for me here, I could have just gone in the cattle car and rode with the cantankerous horse."

Barton lowers his head, as a smirk develops in one corner of his mouth. The visual thought of Smoke spending his first ride on a train with a 'man of the cloth' almost brings his smirk to a full smile.

"Padre, if sitting with me brings you any discomfort, then I will be the one that goes and travels with the grumpy equine in the cattle car. It wouldn't be the first time he has been disgusted with me, and probably won't be the last if we live long enough."

Father Porter chuckles out loud, and waves his hand in the air, as to signal there will not be any need for that. The elderly priest reaches into his time-worn bag, unravels a faded handkerchief, pulls out two pieces of beef jerky, and offers one to his reserved travel companion. After a second of hesitancy, Barton takes the travel staple, from the old man's wrinkled hand, and starts nibbling on it, realizing that he had not taken time for breakfast, and lunch may not be an option in Lawrence if things develop quickly.

"I have read that Jesus was open to breaking bread with many types of people he encountered," the religious cleric started. "I am a little low on the loaf, so this humble piece of smoked meat will have to suffice."

Barton, taking another bite of jerky, responds, "You will have to play the part of Jesus in this little encounter. I am afraid that I will never be confused for the carpenter's son."

Father Porter wraps the remaining piece of his snack in the

handkerchief, places it back in his small tote, and then turns to Barton with a ministerial look on his timeworn face.

"There are very few, in Kansas, that are not aware of what hardships your life has been dealt. And I admit that the newspaper stories and sidewalk chatter have caught my attention, more than once. I guess everyone, in this fine state, has the right to form an opinion, and even go as far as making personal judgments. However I do not have the character traits that elevate me to the status that can make such lofty appraisals. My flock is the only family I have ever known, as I was orphaned upon birth. To share blood with loved ones has got to take one's allegiance and devotion to another level. And to have the darkest corner of Hell reach up and tear them from your life is a devastation that, surely, erupts in a person's heart, takes a turn through the mind, and falls to a man's soul."

Looking back out the window as he tries to figure out where this exchange is going, Barton coldly inquires, "So, you understand what a man has to do when his family is taken from him, and the powers of Heaven stand by and do nothing to stop it?"

Father Porter knows that, as a man of the cloth, he must walk very carefully if he is going to keep this man engaged in a conversation that may be going from introductory to inclusive.

"As I said," the priest begins, "I cannot understand. I have never had the honor of having a blood family. But I sense your question is not in pursuit of my understanding, but my approval. And, that I cannot offer, for the taking of life is as out of my realm as the giving of life. The righteous hand of God must rule in both. The price of error will be paid for a long time. Even in the Bible, men who took life, without ordination from above, never completely walked away from the stain of their impulsive actions. I believe that our Creator works in mysterious ways, His judgments are always right, and He uses men to carry out those judgments. Whether you or others like you, are instruments of divine destiny, surely that will have to be ironed out on a day yet to come, in a court yet to be convened, by an arbitrator far greater than you and I. Don't you think, Mr. Anderson? Mr. Anderson?"

When the elderly priest turned to see why Barton wasn't answering, he discovered that his travel acquaintance wasn't listening to him. Rather, Barton was staring at the front of the railroad car, and his right hand was no longer gripping the barrel of his Henry rifle but was placed on the stock grip, with his index finger on the trigger and the others planted in the cocking lever.

"Mr. Anderson, are we in some sort of ominous predicament that will call for that long gun to be of need during our trip?" Father Porter asked with apprehension swelling in his voice.

Barton did not answer, but slowly moved his stoic gaze from the front of the passenger coach to the back, observing every facial expression for an indication that this wasn't just a casual ride to Lawrence, but that there might be a felonious plan being laid, and who might be the main characters in this dark act of malfeasance.

As he returned his observing eyes to the front of the rail car, Barton moved his hand from the trigger area of the Henry, leaned the rifle back against his chest, and quietly, but firmly starts briefing Father Porter of the situation, "I noticed two men before I got on the train. They seemed to be scoping out the other passengers and their belongings. I can't confirm that, just a feeling in my gut that has worked its way up to my mind. One of them is at the front of the coach, the other is behind us. In the last few minutes, they have been giving each other looks, like they are checking to coordinate some kind of planned action."

The priest, trying not to look around and give away Barton's suspicions, asks, "Do you want me to try to work my way up to the other coach and see if I can find a conductor or another official to share this information with?"

Before Barton could answer, the stranger at the front of the railcar stood up and yelled, "This is a holdup! Start getting your valuables together. When the basket passes by, throw all of them into it! Don't be stupid, there is nothing on this train worth dying for today! And die is what anyone will do if you try to be too brave, there are three guns ready to cut down anyone who tries anything!"

Barton's eyebrows furrowed upon hearing that there were three participants in this villainous act. Sure enough, as he looked around the car, a third bandit stood up. He had been sitting in the middle of the coach, not drawing any attention to himself or looking at the other two that Barton had been watching.

"What are we going to do, Mr. Anderson?" the priest asked, with a tremble in his aged voice.

"What do you mean we?" responded Barton, as he leans the rifle away from his chest and moves it against Father Porter's leg.

As he watches the bandits, in the front and back, hold their handguns on the crowd, Barton notices the third participant starting to work his way to the front of the coach, taking a cane-woven basket with him. The anxiety in the rail car is building and Barton knows he needs to make whatever move he is going to make before others start getting involved, making a difficult situation even that much harder.

Barton took the leather holster strap from the hammer of his .45 Colt, then slowly stood up. Father Porter is now hugging the Henry rifle tightly, in hopes there will be some bravery found in it, somehow.

"Hey, you up front," Barton casually bellows as every head in the car turns in his direction. "I have something I would like to give you!"

The bandit, in the front of the car, gives Barton a perturbed look and instructs him to sit down, so that the basket will make its way back to him soon enough.

"Oh, but you don't understand," Barton continued. "I want to give this to you, personally!"

The robber is now out of patience with the towering man who is sporting a scruffy beard and weather-beaten cowboy hat and is not showing any respect to the fact there is a hold-up going on and he is outnumbered three to one.

"Archie, would you put a bullet in this troublemaker and let's get our haul and get off of this train," the bandit in the front yells, waving his gun in the direction of Barton.

Bang...Bang...Bang!

Screams and yells start rolling through the train car, as the sound of gunfire erupts. Father Porter places his head between his knees, fervently praying as hard as he can, still hugging the Henry rifle as firmly as possible. He is afraid to open his eyes and look around until he hears a familiar voice, coming from beside him...

"Will you move a little, I need to get out and finish this?"

The priest opens one eye, and through the still-hanging cloud of gun smoke, he observes Barton waiting to step out into the aisle. The elderly clergy pushes himself back against the seat, trying to make as much room as he can so his seat neighbor can move past him.

Barton checks on the bandit in the back of the rail car. It was obvious that this one would not be any threat with blood rushing out of a chest wound. As he works his way up the aisle, with people reaching out to shake his hand or pat him on the back, Barton finds another bandit, with his face planted in the basket that he had been gathering stolen goods with. After giving the fallen thief a solid bump with his boot, and getting no response, Barton strolls to the front of the car.

"Oh, my Lord, he is bleeding on me! Get him off of me! He is bleeding on me!" were the screams of a well-dressed lady. The leader of the gang lay in her lap, having fallen on her with the back of his head opened by the exit of a .45 Colt bullet.

"Somebody help me, he is bleeding on me! Lord help me, he is bleeding on my new dress!"

Even when Barton reaches down, grabs the dead bandit by the vest, and pulls him off, the shrill caterwauling continues. Finally, Barton leans over, places his face about six inches from the hysterical woman's face, resolutely looks into her eyes, then softly but firmly inquires,

"Lady, will you shut the hell up?"

As the lady brings her screaming down to a whimpering cry, another sound causes Barton to stand straight up, cock the hammer on his Colt sidearm, and prepare to open fire, again.

Ka-boom!

Barton, frantically, searches the train coach for the source of the sudden gunshot. Within seconds he settles upon a cloud of gun smoke that is working its way out of an open window. As the smoke clears, the source of the gunfire is evident, plainly betrayed by the red face and embarrassed demeanor of the elderly priest. He is still holding the Henry rifle, in a bear hug, as smoke continues to waft out of the barrel.

"I guess I got a little stirred up, by all the gunfire and the screaming. You might want to check the trigger on that cannon, it seems a little sensitive to me."

Barton, shaking his head as he takes the rifle from the priest, continues to shake his head as he looks up and sees the hole that the Henry has put in the roof of the train car. Then, he leans over and whispers into the padre's ear...

"You might want to pass the basket and take up an offering for the roof because I am not paying for that!"

With the Henry rifle under his arm and his saddlebag over his shoulder, Barton turns to walk back to the livestock car, where he will finish this trip with the only living creature that he truly trusts and welcomes the company of...Smoke.

2

———

As soon as the train slows to a stop, Barton opens the cattle car gate and lets it fall to the unloading dock, providing a convenient ramp for him, and Smoke, to disembark off of the locomotive. Once he secures his saddle bag in place and slides the Henry rifle into its sheath, he mounts upon Smoke and turns to start the next stage of his mission…to find Angus Ford's sister.

"Surely you were not going to leave without saying goodbye, Mr. Anderson!"

Barton turns to see Father Porter standing beside the train, his humble travel bag in one hand, and the other hand extended in an upward stance, toward the mounted Barton.

"I would love to say it has been a complete pleasure meeting you and traveling with you," the elderly priest starts. "But the only thing I am sure of is that it wasn't boring, and it wasn't something I will be forgetting for quite a while."

Barton smirks, coerces Smoke to move over toward the old parson, and says, "If nothing else, you now have a story to tell the kids at that orphanage. You can tell them how you helped foil a holdup on a train, and you even got a shot off. Just don't mention which direction the bullet went in. That will take a lot of the bravado out of the tale of Father Porter, gun-toting padre."

As the white-haired man lets out a hearty laugh, Barton reaches down and takes the priest's hand, shakes it firmly, and nods his head in a way to confirm that the experience has been one that he will remember for a while, too.

With the urging of a well-placed heel and the pulling of the reins, Smoke spins around and starts to leave again, but another unforeseen voice causes Barton to pull firmly back on the reins, which stops the long-legged horse, and his rider, in their tracks, again.

"Sir, I don't think you will be going anywhere until we have an official chat about what happened on this train today!"

Barton, not recognizing the husky voice, slides his right hand down to the elkhorn handle of his .45 Colt. He, slowly, turns in the saddle to where he can see the stranger while presenting himself as a difficult target, in case this meeting has a clandestine cause as its motive. Even though the first thing Barton notices is the five-point star on the man's chest, he does not lessen his grip on his handgun.

"Mister, there are too many people, in this train station area, to initiate an ill-advised confrontation. Plus, my deputy is to your immediate right, has a trustworthy rifle aimed at your right shoulder, and if you even think of pulling your gun, scratching your head, or wiping your brow, you will spend the rest of your life learning to do things better with your left hand. Do you understand, Mr. Anderson?"

Barton is starting to get perplexed at the fact that, for a trip that was planned so he could arrive in Lawrence unnoticed, every person he has spoken to has seemed to know who he is.

"Ok, Sheriff," the stoic man on the gray horse starts. "I am going to slide my hand around and put it in the back of my gun belt, to show that I am not going to make any moves, yet. I would imagine you have a pre-selected signal to let your law partner know that things are under control for now."

As Barton takes his hand off of the Colt pistol and places it behind him, the lawman points a finger at the deputy, waves the digit in a downward motion, and the sheriff's legal sidekick lowers his Winchester rifle to his waist, not ready to relax his watch on the target, still sitting on Smoke.

"I am Clifton Massey, the sheriff of Douglas County, in which Lawrence is the county seat. The prospective sharp-shooter, standing on the loading dock, is Deputy Punch Phillips. He doesn't talk much, kind of leaves that obligation to me. Punch is a 'people watcher', and he doesn't miss a whole lot, doesn't waste time, doesn't squander opportunities, and doesn't abuse the county's ammunition budget by missing very often. I think I have established our standing around here. Would you say that you have enough information to ensure that you will be making very wise decisions for the next 15 minutes?"

Barton looks at the lawman and makes a gesture with his hand to inquire if it's safe for him to get down. The sheriff nods to the affirmative, and Barton slowly gets off of Smoke, while still holding his hand inside the back of his gun belt, mindful of the rules that the local lawman has austerely laid down.

"I am here because of a telegram I got earlier," Sheriff Massey continues. "It came from U.S. Marshal Lyndon Tomes. It stated that an acquaintance of his was coming to Lawrence, why this person was coming, and that this acquaintance would need help in locating someone quickly. Mr. Anderson, I respected Marshal Tomes until a little while ago. The fact he is willing to associate with you causes me pause in my judgment of him. And, let there be no doubt of my judgment of you. In my line of work, I don't suffer bounty hunters, avenging angels, or whatever the hell you are. You make good people nervous, you make bad people more nervous. And, when people get nervous, they do very stupid things, things that cause me to be inconvenienced. And I am not a nice guy when I am inconvenienced. If you don't believe me, just ask Deputy Phillips over there. He has seen me when I am not feeling satisfied with how my daily schedule is unfolding."

Barton turns, slightly, in the direction of the deputy, who has not moved one inch since he was ordered to lower his Winchester weapon. Time is a valuable commodity, and he is growing weary of this presentation of who is the top dog, in this town, on this day. Barton turns back toward the sheriff and decides it's time to stop the aggressive posturing and get to the reason why he is here.

"I don't care what you think of me, Marshal Tomes, the weather or anything else. If you know why I am here, then the more information you give me, the faster I will be out of your jurisdiction and the faster you can go back to being a nice lawman, having a nice day."

Father Porter, who has been standing on the railroad dock, observes that Barton is being pushed beyond the barrier of his limited self-restraint, much like the bandits did on the train. The cleric steps up to the sheriff, introduces himself, and proceeds to tell the story of how Barton kept a bad situation from getting worse, diffused it quickly, and kept any passengers from suffering harm or worse. Sheriff Massey says he appreciates the padre's account of the events and says that the 'man of the cloth' should be a little more particular about the company he is seen with and is willing to speak up for.

Before the priest can respond to the lawman's rebuke, Barton takes a step toward the sheriff, which causes the deputy to raise his rifle again. Even though he doesn't see the offensive stance the junior lawman has taken, Barton hears the Winchester rifle scrape against the metal badge on the deputy's chest. Plus, he detects Smoke making a low nickering sound and shuffling his front hooves. Barton knows that is indicative that his equine travel partner has had his limit of the cocky theatrics being spouted off, at the expense of time, which is not an asset the towering man has.

"Sheriff," Barton cooly, but firmly, responds. "I don't have the time for you to piss on every tree in this town, marking your territory like an excited coonhound with a bad bladder. Neither do I have the luxury of interrupting my schedule to fill out paperwork explaining why I had to shoot two of Douglas County's finest peace officers. You, simply, tell me where I can find Angus Ford's sister, and there will be no one happier for me to leave than me."

At some point during this unfolding confrontation, Father Porter has closed his eyes, folded his hands, and has slipped into emergency intercession for the deteriorating detente between the two men before him. Sheriff Massey, surmising that it would be better to leave the scene alive than buy a moral victory with someone's blood, gestures to Deputy Phillips to walk away. Then, the chief lawman lays his rifle against a barrel containing carpenter nails, unbuckles his gun belt, and lets it fall to the ground. Father Porter looks up at the heavens and mouths a silent 'thank you' as the scowl on Barton's face starts to ease a bit.

"I have heard a lot of things about you, shooter," the sheriff says. "But nothing that would cause me to deduce that you are a man who would take the life of an unarmed person. But I guess I could just be under-informed, and I could have just made the last mistake of my life. Are we going to come to a peaceable, working resolution of why you need me?"

Barton hooks his thumbs in the belt loops on his faded

jeans, leans back against Smoke, and answers the sheriff, with his usual steely stare and unflappable demeanor.

"I just need one thing from you. Information. And if you don't have it, then I will, discreetly, move on to the next possible source. One thing is for sure, I am not leaving Lawrence until I secure what I came for. You have my word that I have no intention to shoot or kill anyone. But, lawman, know that I will not hesitate if either of those options help remove any obstacle to my intended purpose of coming to Lawrence. Now, if we have that peaceable, working resolve that you were speaking of, then let's get to work. Where can I find Angus Ford's sister, sheriff?"

Sheriff Massey hops up on the barrel full of carpenter nails, sits back, and exhales slowly. Then he speaks in a matter-of-fact cadence, where Barton and Father Porter can hear every detail.

"You are looking for Beatrice Wingmire. She dumped the family name a few years ago because it seemed to get in the way of her pursuing a profitable profession. But most people still know her as 'Big Bea' and using that moniker will get you farther, and faster, in your inquiries. Trying to be as delicate as I can be, in front of the parson, Big Bea is in the entertainment business, if you get my drift. A busy house on the same street as the big saloons, a handful of enticingly dressed ladies as tenants, and a lot of smiling gentlemen leaving in the late hours paints the picture of where you will be and who you will be around."

"Does she have any protection for this entertainment business?" Barton asks, as he intently contemplates every word that the lawman has shared.

Sheriff Massey pretends to be offended by Barton's question, then goes straight to making sure all the cards are on the table, especially in Barton's mind.

"If you are asking if the sheriff of Douglas County is benefitting from Big Bea's profitable establishment, the answer is a straight no. The simple understanding, that my office has with the large lady, is if all of her customers remain happy, under control, and the noise is manageable, then that part of town will never see us. It's the same agreement we have with the saloons and gambling houses. But, if just one customer comes to me bitching, bleeding, or with their pockets involuntarily emptied, then we chain the doors shut, nail the windows fast, and wait for the district judge to hold court to rule on when they can expect to re-open. And seeing that the wheels of justice turn slow in Lawrence, that 'profitable' status starts shrinking fast in the back office. Does that answer your question, Mr. Anderson?"

Barton, with a frown on his face, responds, "Actually, when I asked if Ms. Wingmire had protection, I was thinking more of the large, goon-looking type, with biceps bigger than their brains. But I assure you that the padre, and I, will sleep well knowing that we are under the trustworthy care of the very virtuous Douglas County sheriff's office. Isn't that right, parson?"

The lawman chuckles at Barton's assessment of his morals and talents and then cackles out loud when he turns to Father Porter and notices that the cleric's eyes are as big as the coffee cup saucers at the downtown diner. The priest was not ready for this candid indoctrination to his new ministry field, but he knew that there would always be multi-faceted people in need of his religious gifts, no matter where he went. Father Porter takes a big breath and then signals for the sheriff to continue.

Sheriff Massey turns back to Barton and recommences with his quick lesson on life in Lawrence, Kansas.

"Big Bea employs various helpers with the daily keeping of the facilities, but she has three such characters, as you describe, and they have one function at Big Bea's place, to hurt people who get out of hand. That's it, simple and to the point. These roughnecks have no ability to reason with you, to play politics with you, nor will they ever be mistaken for the padre here. They are on the payroll to handle, hurt, and then hide the results from everyone who could care, including God, himself. Big man, you had better be as good as the stories make you out to be, because if you are not, then this will be the last time I will ever have to worry about you being in my county."

Barton steps toward Smoke, gets up in the saddle, looks at the lawman, and says, "Then, no matter what may be waiting at Ms. Wingmire's, no matter how it turns out, there is a chance this is going to be a good day for you, and your schedule will not be too interrupted."

The lawman laughs, then gets a look on his face, as if he has just remembered another piece of pressing information that needs to be resolved before Barton leaves.

"If the train robbers, you conveniently killed today, are who I think they are, I am sure they have rewards, on their heads, for arrest or demise. That is rightfully yours, so where should I send the funds to?"

Barton wrinkles his brow in thought, looks down at Smoke, strokes the horse's powerful neck with his hand, then asks his equine friend a question that takes those who are listening by surprise, "Are you thinking what I am thinking, boy?" The gray horse appears to shake his head in agreement with whatever Barton has surmised. The answer to Sheriff Massey's question comes as an even bigger shock.

"Lawman, so that you don't ever have to dirty your hands, or badge, with me again, I am told that there is a modest orphanage in this place that is getting a new overseer. If this person doesn't have any problems with how the money was raised, then make an anonymous contribution to the kids. Can't do a damn thing about how you and I wound up, but maybe we can assist the padre with molding future citizens."

Barton glances, quickly, at Father Porter and notices that the aging clergyman has tears welling up in his eyes, his hands folded in a pose of gratitude, and the padre, once more, softly mouths the words, "Thank you."

Barton places his heels against Smoke's sides, and instructs his animal friend that it is time to go, and Smoke starts trotting away from the train station. Over the sound of the people talking, the train steam releasing, and the sound of Smoke's hooves hitting the ground, Barton hears one more utterance from Sheriff Massey.

"Hey, shooter, if I don't ever hear from you again, I hope it doesn't hurt your feelings if I don't care and don't come looking for you!"

If this was one last chance for the cavalier lawman to 'pee on another tree', as Barton put it, it didn't get a response. The tall man's mind is already considering what may be awaiting him and how many more encounters will he have to experience before he gets to the one that really matters...confirming that Seth is still alive.

3

Barton has discovered, while on his covert travels across Kansas, that it is not too hard to find out where the liquor, ladies, loudmouths, and lucky card chasers converge. Actually, the chances are better that you will hear the evidence before you see the signs of where the laughs are cheap, the love can be bartered, and life hangs in the balance of a cross look or a crooked hand of stud poker. Locating Big Bea's business can wait, for the real action won't pick up for a few hours. For now, Barton will search for a place for him, and Smoke, to find some nourishment.

After asking a young, vociferous paperboy where the nearest livery stable was, Barton got back on Smoke and headed in that direction. Although Barton had been on the outskirts of Lawrence while tracking one of his barbaric targets, he had never been in the midst of the city. Three facets of his focus on operating was to know your mark, know your location, and know your route of escape. More than once, Barton had escaped calamity by being able to 'retreat and regroup' when a confrontation was interrupted by unforeseen circumstances or unwitting participants. He had always remembered one of the first things that Marshal Tomes had told him, "Being impatient or unprepared will get you killed eventually." Today, he will not deviate from the mindset that has kept him alive, so far.

The commotion level of Lawrence, this day, did not seem to be extraordinarily hectic or festive. Unlike Topeka, which was always bustling with business, government, legalities, and other affairs, 'another day on the plains' could describe Lawrence, at any given time. The area had its share of ranchers, farmers, loggers, miners, and the like. Therefore, the town was comprised of businesses and traders that would strive to keep all of these enterprises going. So, Barton just let Smoke move at his own pace, while he made mental notes of the main streets, alleys, side paths, and spaces that just happened to be there, due to poor planning or property lines.

As Smoke sauntered along, only changing his direction when he felt his rider pull the reins against his neck, Barton never got off his easy-gaited friend. He thought it was funny that there was an accepted truth about being a stranger in a bigger town. If you were observed riding in alleys, or behind buildings, most people would just think you had made an erroneous tack in your route. But, for some reason, if you were discovered to be walking, alone, in those same sectors, then suspicion was raised as to what your intentions were. So, Barton just took in the prospects of future movements, both intentional and in unexpected peril.

When they had ambled for an hour or so, Barton observed what could be the livery stable that the paperboy had given him directions to. Once they were within a couple of hundred feet or so, Barton listened for the sound of a hammer hitting steel, or some other smithy's noise that would further establish that this was where they needed to be. Within moments, a young black male, maybe twenty or so in age, came out of a side door, carrying a large sack of corn grain over his shoulder. He leaned forward, letting the large burlap bag fall to the ground. The sound of Smoke's hooves clopping against the hard ground, finally, got the muscular laborer's attention, resulting in him rubbing his hands together and flashing a smile that gave Barton the impression that he had found, at least, one friendly face in Lawrence.

"You the owner of this fine business establishment?" Barton asks with a straight look on his face, pretty sure of the answer that would soon be coming.

The young man chuckled and responded, "Only when I am laying in the shade, with my eyes closed, dreaming about a future that would allow me to have an outfit of my own. Today, I am just manual labor, sweating for the one who does operate this place. Who knows, one day that name over the main door just might be mine, if I work hard enough, save enough and the breaks fall in my favor. Yes sir, might just see it up there, someday."

Barton gets down off of Smoke, walks over to where the young dreamer is standing, and asks, "And what name will be over that door, if those fortunate breaks line up in your favor?"

With a growing smile spreading across his honest, perspiring face, he responds, "Isaac Mayes' Livery and Feed Store, that is what it will say. I like the ring of that, don't you, sir?"

A corner of Barton's mouth turns up in a grin of appreciation for the young man's passion to dream, and his vision of what might be. For a brief moment, listening to this youthful optimist takes Barton back to when he was about this age, how he and Jenny would sit up on Rooster Pass and talk about what their future would look like, how big their family would be, and naming their home 'Anderson Ranch'. But Barton never let such reminiscences linger, for he knew the heart-tugging reminders would soon give way to the heart-breaking realities.

"What is the chance of my hungry friend getting feed and water, plus keeping an eye on my tack for the next few hours?" Barton asks, as he moves his mind back to why he is in Lawrence.

"Two bits will get you all of that, and I will even provide your famished friend with the pleasure of some of my favorite musical offerings, to help him pass the time while you are gone," Isaac said, his ever-present smile never fading.

Barton reaches into his pocket, pulls out four bits, gently tosses them to the young livery worker, and states, "Here, treat him as if he was your horse, and he like waltzes, seems to keep him calmer than barn dance numbers. They tend to rile him up, and that is the last thing you want, trust me."

Barton leads Smoke into the barn structure, takes the saddle off of the back of the big gray, and places it on the stable wall where Smoke will stay. Also placed with the saddle are Barton's saddle bags and his Henry rifle, still in its sheath. For now, he is figuring that his Colt sidearm will be adequate for his continued hunt for Angus Ford's sister.

Isaac grabs a bucket, and fills it with a mixture of oats and corn. The sound of the kernels hitting the bottom of the metal bucket causes Smoke's ears to perk up, and the thought of his first food of the day prompts his eager feet to start skittering on the dirt floor. After checking that his equine visitor had plenty of water to go with his meal, the young livery worker turned to Barton. The tall man was going thru something, in his saddle bag, that he might need later.

"Sir, what brings you to Lawrence? Do you have specific business or are you just passing through to another place? If you have a need for directions or suggestions, I am pretty familiar with this town. I was born and raised here, and I will include that service as a compliment to the funds you have already compensated me for, so far."

Barton suppresses a small chuckle as he listens to this young, prospective entrepreneur working on his trade skills. He finishes going through his saddle bag, places some items in his pockets, and then places one arm upon his saddle, which is sitting astride the stall where Smoke is, energetically, enjoying his filling meal.

"I am in town looking for someone, need to get to them as soon as possible. But I don't think they will be available until later this evening. So, I think I will be like my four-legged friend here, and go find me some grub to savor, and just pass the time until the hour is right to further my errand."

Isaac is now sharing the stock food mixture with a couple of other horses that are in a nearby stall. Once he empties the bucket, he throws it aside and walks over to where Barton is standing, and continues his overture to help the rugged visitor with his purpose and his plans.

"As for eating, you can find a lot of choices if you just head straight up Maple Street there. Just depends on what you feel like, can't go wrong with any of them. Well, except for that new Asian place. I haven't ate there yet, but you wouldn't believe what some people are saying they serve there. They say you don't want to know what those strange words on the menu really say. You ever heard such a thing, mister?"

Barton, again, stifles the urge to snicker, in response to his young travel guide's brutal, but innocent, impression of this latest eatery. Barton assures him that he will be looking for the normal staple of 'meat and potatoes', then just relax and wait for the hands on the clock to move forward to a convenient time to resume his task.

"If you can give me any clues as to what you are looking for, I am sure I could help you with finding this meaningful place you are in search of."

Barton looks off into the mass of buildings, pauses to consider if he wants to involve this young man in his endeavors, then decides to let the cards fall where they may.

"You know where I can find a business that is run by a woman named 'Big Bea'? It's supposed to be right in the saloon district?"

Isaac's bright smile disappears and is replaced by a look of disappointment, mixed with a touch of disdain. Barton now wonders if he has made a mistake and gone too far, in his discourse with the young livery worker.

"Sir, that is not a very nice place. I have a pretty good idea what goes on behind that big yellow door on the front of the building," Isaac starts. "I know that ever since I was a kid, my momma told me she would wear out a willow switch, on my behind, if she ever caught me just sitting on the front stoop of Big Bea's place."

Barton, while still wondering if initiating this conversation was the right move, looks back at Isaac and attempts to reassure the bewildered young man that his desires, to enter the building with the yellow door, did not involve the normal services that Big Bea was known for, especially around Lawrence.

"I am looking for information about how I can find someone. That's all. I don't have time to waste on floozies, booze, losers, and whatever else can be found there."

Isaac, still trying to mentally regroup from Barton's desire to visit such a disreputable establishment, shakes his head and waves his hand, in a manner that he was no longer interested in helping Barton while he was in Lawrence. He turns to continue with his chores in the livery, and Barton finds that even though he is losing time, the fact he has lost Isaac's respect has become important to him.

"Isaac, some very evil gunmen took my youngest son. There is a chance that Ms. Wingmire knows where he is. I have got to find him, he is all I have left. Can you understand I don't want to go up there, but I have to. And I will find it, even if you or anyone else in this town refuses to help me."

Isaac pauses what he is doing. As he stands there, he gets a look on his face like his mind is being bombarded by details, thoughts, and possibilities. Then, as his countenance is gripped by a growing realization, the young livery worker stares at Smoke, moves his eyes to the Henry rifle, and turns his head, slowly, back in the direction where Barton is standing. Like lightning hitting a tall oak tree, Isaac's eyes open wide, his lips spread slightly, and his arm rises as he points his finger at the tall man before him. Like a runaway train rolling out of a tunnel, a verbal affirmation bursts out of his mouth.

"You're him! You're that man my momma has been talking about, the one who lost all of his family in Smithview! I can't remember your name, but you killed all those who did it, didn't you? You are the man on the gray horse, with the Henry rifle! Oh, my Lordy! Are you going to kill me?"

Barton says nothing, letting his new acquaintance process all that is running through his unsettled mind. He doesn't know what Isaac has heard, whether it is truth or fairytales. Barton leans against a barn post, crosses his arms, and waits for Isaac to show where this critical moment is taking them.

Isaac is trying to comprehend what his next move should be, but his thoughts are whirling like an afternoon dust devil. First, he talks to himself, then he converses with a nearby pitchfork and even seems to consult Smoke for guidance. The whole time, Barton continues to bide his time, hoping that the perplexed young man can find a resolution to this startling epiphany. When Isaac doesn't seem to be able to firmly grasp his bearings,

Barton decides to take a chance on bringing things back to where they were.

"Isaac, I am Barton Anderson, let's get that out in the open. I am not here to kill anyone, that is not my plan. I am here, as I said, to try to find my son. His name is Seth. I haven't seen him in a long time. I need your help, if you can find it in you. But, if you can't, I will keep searching on my own. One thing is for sure, I can't wait any longer."

After a few more moments of silence, Barton turns and starts to walk out of the stable, resolved that he is on his own, again. But Isaac, while still feeling apprehensive about getting involved with a man of such a reputation, works up the words that will cause Barton to halt his long strides away from the livery.

"I will help you, sir. I don't want to be a part of anyone getting killed or nothing. But if a little boy is in trouble, then I can point you in the right direction. Do you think he is up there in that awful place with all those wicked goings on?"

Barton turns, takes a big breath, lets it out slowly, then responds to Isaac's inquiry.

"I don't know. Maybe he is, and it will just be a matter of taking him away from them and going home. But, I have been told of another possibility that will mean this is only a place to start. No matter, I will find my boy, and will do what I have to. If that bothers you, then get back to your work and I will get on with mine."

Isaac walks to the front doors of the livery, points toward the outside, and starts, "You go up this street here, for about two blocks. Then you will turn left on what's called Clover Street. Go down that one until you see a big streetlight, later it will be shining like a full moon on a fall night. That's the Silver Way, called that because if you don't have any silver or other money, you ain't going to be able to join in the action found on both sides of the street. Big Bea's place is halfway down on the left. Can't miss it, just look for the yellow door."

Barton walks outside, stopping to contemplate what his next actions will be. Then, he turns back in the direction of the young livery keeper and says, "You haven't done a bad thing by helping me. All I want is my boy, and you have just helped me know where to look. If anything else happens, you didn't have anything to do with that. As I said, I would have found the place no matter what, no matter the circumstances."

"Do you think there will be trouble?" Isaac asks, with a tone of concern for the vigilant father's wellbeing.

"Don't know," Barton answers. "These are people who took another man's son. If Seth is there, I don't know what they are willing to do to keep him. But I know what I am willing to do to get him back. If I don't return for the horse, you will know that there was more trouble than I anticipated or could respond to."

Realizing that that could be a regrettable outcome, Isaac asks, "What do I do with the gray horse, if the sun comes up and he is still standing in the stall waiting for you?"

With a smirk forming in the corner of his mouth, Barton looks at Smoke and replies, "If he is here long enough, you will find that he doesn't stay anywhere he doesn't cotton to. If I don't turn up, he will make his way out of your barn and will find his way home. Pretty hard-headed, that way. He doesn't need me near as much as I need him."

"I say you come back, later on, and introduce me to this fine young man, named Seth. He must be a good one for you to walk into all that unknown mess alone," Isaac requests.

Barton tips the brim of his hat, and as he turns to start his trek to the Silver Way, he responds, "I am going, not just because he is a fine young man, but because he is an Anderson."

4

As afternoon gives way to evening, Barton sits at a front window table in a corner café. The Angry Bull restaurant is, literally, on the corner of Clover Street and Silver Way. Having long finished his meal, Barton has used the advantageous location, and time, to observe the change in daylight and the mood of the social climate in Lawrence. Earlier, most of the traffic could be described as 'business beneficial', as in deliveries being made, employees arriving for duties and casual participants of the services being offered at that time. Now, Barton has noticed that the steps are getting faster, the voices are getting louder, and the facial expressions are getting hopeful as the change is made to 'entertainment essential', where after-dark rendezvous with gambling, girls, and gossip fodder will be the rule of love and life until the sun comes up on another day.

With the waitress content to keep his coffee cup filled, Barton has used this time to ponder the possibilities that this night might hold. Until he, actually, sees Big Bea's establishment, he won't be able to purpose a plan of action. For now, his diligent mind is running around one question that could have an impact on the entire effort. It is a consideration that is real and must be kept in a place of focus, or this could all end in failure. That question is: Will he be able to stay sharp, and on point if Seth is there? It has been over a year since he has seen his youngest child. Will the sight of his last living family member be too much to keep control of his emotions? Up to now, Barton could always rely on revenge, hate, and vindication to restrain his disposition. He had mastered the state of cold-heartedness. The time for emotional reunions and realities will be for another day. Tonight is about finding and recovering.

Another prospect had, also, been trying to work its way into Barton's consciousness, one that he had refused to even consider until the last hour or so. What if Coy Newton had lied about Seth still being alive? What if the revelation was just a dying outlaw's last stab in the heart of his killer? Barton had never put any credence into the words of a murderous fugitive, never gave one an ounce of credibility. But this was a different situation, a more intimate consideration. If Newton has lied, then Barton can live with the disappointment of an empty attempt. He, resolutely, knows that he could never live with not trying, and then someday finding out that Seth had been out there, all along, wondering why his daddy never came.

After another thirty minutes pass, Barton stands up and places enough money on the table to pay the bill and show his appreciation to the waitress. Then, he turns and walks out onto The Silver Way. The night air is already filling up with the celebratory howls of winners, the angry curses of losers, the encouraging calls for new players, and the seductive promises of helping losers forget their losses with another drink. The smell of cheap liquor and old beer hangs over the street, like an intrusive fog. The aroma of alcohol had never been an attraction to

Barton, for the largest part of his life, because of moral reasons. Now, the reason is for survival purposes, as alcohol can make the smartest man an idiot, and the fastest gun slow enough to never be drawn again. Barton, suddenly, stops walking and takes a big breath, for he sees his destination for this night. The yellow door of Big Bea's den of distraction and decadence.

Barton decides to move across the street and monitor the situation from there. So, he leans up against a hitching rail and gets comfortable for the task. His first observation was that Big Bea's attracted all kinds of men, from the tall, handsome, and well-dressed to the short, dumpy, and plainly attired. In a place like this, everyone gets treated like social royalty, if you have the money. It didn't take long for Barton to determine that going in the front was not going to be an option. One of the big goons, that the sheriff had spoken of, has been stationed outside the front door. This oaf was not a social meet and greet agent but was there to relieve anyone of a gun that they might be carrying. His style was rough and to the point, not even giving the surprised patron a chance to announce they were packing. Each fellow received a rough patting down, then the big ruffian would run his bear-paw sized hands into their coats, shirts, pockets, or anywhere he might have thought he felt a weapon. Once removed, the gun was thrown into a nearby box, and the patron was directed to go on in. If anyone protested the act of the search or seizure of their weapon, the result was a violent fist to the gut, then being propelled to the cobblestone street without the benefit of the stairs. No, Barton needed to make his entrance as quietly as possible, so another route would need to be found.

After strolling around the building, Barton found what could be his best way of gaining access to the inside of Big Bea's. A delivery wagon, arriving with a load of liquor, presented itself just as Barton walked into the back alley. If he timed this just right, he would let the lone laborer take in the first case of drinks. Then, Barton would slip up to the wagon, pick up a box of bottled spirits, place it on his shoulder, so as to hide his face from observation. If he pulls this off, he should be able to walk right into the festive place. Being a tall man, the bottom of his coat would pull down over his gun, allowing him to enter into this unknown territory with his Colt revolver undetected.

Barton was, slightly, surprised at how easily his plan went off, as he strolled into the building without any resistance. He laid the box of booze down, at the first convenient place, and walked into what had to be the main parlor. Men were sitting around the room, drinking, chatting, and waiting for their moment. As Barton sized up the lively surroundings, a brightly dressed girl walked up to him, asking if he had anyone in mind or if was he up for new company tonight.

Barton answered, "Yeah, I have someone in mind. I would like to see the head whore."

The young girl gasped, surprised at the steely man's response and his blunt manner. Once she regained her composure, she explained to him that Ms. Wingmire was not available, but that she was sure that there was an enchanting girl who would be willing to help him, whatever that might be.

Barton steps closer to the young lady, leans forward to where his eyes are in line with hers, with a look that has frozen many in their tracks and says with a cold tone, "No, I want to see the head whore of this establishment."

When Barton saw the young lady's eyes leave him and look over his shoulder, he knew that this confrontation was no longer just the two of them. The smell of bad breath hit him before the thug's antagonistic words did.

"Mister, I think you and I need to take a leisurely walk outside and talk about your piss-poor attitude, maybe even help you adjust it."

When Barton turned around, he was facing a barbarian that

was, probably, four inches taller than him and was a good two hundred pounds heavier. With one quick motion, Barton pulled his revolver and drove the seven-and-a-half-inch barrel into the huge bouncer's stomach twice, causing the house bully to bend over in pain. With his adversary in a compromised position, Barton raised the Colt sidearm high in the air and brought the elkhorn handle down across the back of the brute's neck, causing him to fall into a large human lump at Barton's feet. The rest of the parlor was quiet and motionless, no one willing to draw Barton's attention to them.

Barton, with no expression on his face, turned to the young lady, who is trembling and in fear of the man in front of her. He says only one word, but everyone knows what he means.

"Now!"

As the girl turns to try to meet Barton's request, a door opens, and a heavy-set mature woman steps out. She is dressed in a manner that would announce that she is of stature and status, and the attention, that the other females are giving her, makes Barton feel like this is who he has come to see.

"Get in here, cowboy! I can't have you ruining the festive atmosphere that I have spent so much time, effort, and money to establish. Let these fine people relax their lungs and continue with what they are here for. You and I can discuss your despicable way of getting my attention in private."

Barton puts his Colt back in its holster, steps around the fallen bruiser, and follows the seasoned woman into what is, probably, her office. Even though she implores him to have a seat, Barton chooses to remain standing, with one eye on the only door in the room. The woman pours herself a drink, and offers one to her aloof guest, which he waves off. Then she sits in the padded chair behind the desk. After giving Barton a once over, she starts her inquiry.

"I am referred to as Ms. Wingmire, not the head whore.

What in the world could be so important that you have to come in here and scare the life out of my hostess, and then beat the hell out of one of my entertainment directors? Sir, your civilities are greatly lacking, and will not be tolerated in this establishment, any longer. You make your case and then get out, or you will be thrown out!"

Barton responds, calmly but confidently, "I want my boy back."

Ms. Wingmire laughs, slaps her hands on the desk, and proclaims, "There have been a lot of boys that have come in here and left as men. I can't do a thing about any life-changing experience your impressionable boy might have had while he was here. If I had a name or a description, I might remember this young shaver who became an adult at The Pleasure Palace."

Not showing any emotion or expression, Barton answered, "His name is Seth. Your brother, Angus, brought him here, after taking him from my ranch. Give him to me, and there will be no more trouble, plain as that."

The laughing woman is no longer laughing, her jovial disrespect has been replaced by an alternating look of anger and fear. She reaches for a drawer in the desk, but when Barton lowers his hand to his Colt revolver, she draws her hand back. With her eyes shooting daggers at the man in front of her, she growls, "He said you would come. You are the bastard that killed my brothers and my cousin. You are a dead man. Max, Jimmy, get in here!"

Within seconds of yelling for help, the office door flies open, and two large thugs attempt to come to the aid of their boss. But they don't even get their guns raised or their feet in the door.

Bang! Bang!

Both hooligans fall to the floor, with the force of a large river rock being thrown off a bridge. Barton turns his gun toward the gasping woman, smoke still trailing out of the blue-steeled barrel. He walks around the desk, places the end of the barrel against her shaking forehead, then shares a bit of information to help her know that he is at the end of his patience.

"This is where my gun was when I blew your rotten brother's brains out. If you don't tell me what I want to know, and do it within the next breath you take, then I will decorate the wall behind you with the insides of your head. I am in the mood to rid this world of another Ford, and that is what you are, Ms. Wingmire. Tell me where my son is, you over-the-hill hustler!"

With the realization that she has no other play, and the man with the gun has a reputation for leaving a trail of people who thought they knew better, she responds.

"It doesn't matter, rancher. You see, I have the pleasure of knowing that you don't have a snowball's chance in hell of ever getting your boy back. It doesn't matter how bad people say that you are, or how good you are with that gun. You will never see your boy again."

Barton pulls the hammer back, on the Colt six-shooter, and pushes the barrel tighter against the forehead of the suddenly impudent woman. With his eyes squinting and his eyebrows narrowing, Barton calmly says, "Say hi to Angus when you get to hell."

"No! No! No! Wait! I will tell you!" Her brashness rapidly dissolves in the reality that seeing her dead brother is not a priority, but living is.

With the gun cocked and still positioned against her trembling brow, the information that Barton is seeking rolls out of the heavy-set woman, like maple syrup in the fall. She tells of how Angus Ford brought this boy to her and said the kid was an orphan and wouldn't be missed. He said that, surely, some of my rich patrons would pay good money for a kid, especially if their old ladies weren't capable of giving them one. So, she started dropping small hints here and there, that she had the ability to fix that problem if any prospective fathers were serious. After a few days, she got an anonymous note from someone, saying that they knew of such a rich, but childless couple. They had plenty of cash to pay for a kid. But if it ever became public, serious harm would come to those who spilled it.

"Where is Seth, during this whole time?" Barton asks, becoming more captivated by the story, but not lowering the Colt pointed at Big Bea.

"Oh, we took good care of him, I promise," Bea answers, trying to ease the tension a bit, and not stir Barton up anymore. "The little fellow was sick from a snake bite, but we nursed him the best we could. The girls loved the kid, he was treated like a prince around here. But you can't keep a little kid around a place like this, and I had some belated bills that needed paying, so I waited to be contacted, and I was eventually."

Barton, lowering the gun, but still keeping it directed in her direction, urges Bea to continue.

"It was a late Friday night, we were in the process of closing up when there was a knock on the front door. When we told them that we would open again tomorrow, they stated that they were here for the boy and had money to make it happen. I opened the door, and there stood a fine-dressed man holding a fancy business case. He walked in, we brought the kid out, he grabbed a wad of money from the case, asked if that would be enough, I gave him the kid and they left. Haven't seen them since."

Barton, now, has a perplexed look on his face, and asks, "You let a kid leave with a total stranger, in the middle of the night? No questions asked? I ought to kill you for that!"

Bea shakes her head, looks at Barton, and sheepishly responds, "Hey, people who have a lot of money are never strangers, just friends we have never met, yet. I, actually, found out who he was later, and got mad I didn't ask for more money.

Real rich guy, one of my girls recognized him from when she worked in a Topeka party house."

Barton can feel his heart beating a little faster, as the thought of being able to narrow his search down to a name, and a place, brings him one step closer to finding Seth.

"Who was this mysterious man in the night, this buyer of children?" Barton quizzes, trying not to lose his focus on who is telling this story, or letting her relax from her sense of urgency.

"The guy's name is Henry Livingston. I am told that he is a very rich, very powerful businessman in Topeka. He is a big player in real estate, the railroad, oil, lumber, and some business interests that are not exactly above board, if you know what I mean. He likes being rich and is willing to play rough to keep his lifestyle. And to make sure he is always holding all the winning cards, he has a list, as long as his arm, of politicians, lawmen, and gunslingers that he pays for their loyalty. Rancher, you can forget ever seeing that boy of yours. I also hear that Livingston's old lady had always wanted a child, but couldn't have one on her own. So Livingston bought her one. I guess she's happy, and he wants to keep her that way. It looks good in the social circles and political parties, you know. That's why I said you ain't got a snowball's chance in hell of ever seeing that boy. You are one bad man, one fast gun, that's it. He is a vicious son-of-a-bitch who has the law, the government, and an army of guns to squash you, like a bug. You need to go home, find yourself a nice, new wife, and start a new family. No matter how you try to look at it, your first family is gone."

Barton, unmoved by the big woman's dire account of his chances, puts his gun back in its holster and says, "One truth about snakes, cut its head off and the rest of it will die. I just have to find the snake and put a bullet through its head. Simple as that."

Big Bea chuckles, looks over Barton's shoulder, and then

proclaims, "You have one problem, big man. You will have to live long enough to get to Topeka. And I don't think you are going to live long enough to get out of this room. You see, you killed two of my entertainment directors, but the third one is standing in the door, with a gun pointed right at you. I know you are fast with that Colt, but I am betting you can't turn and fire before he puts, at least, one bullet into your heathen back. So, you can say hi to my brother when YOU get to hell!"

Barton takes a slow breath, his mind racing over what he must do to have a chance against a gun that is already pulled and pointed at him. Just when he accepts what seems to be his only move, and his muscles tense to respond to mental demands, he hears a peculiar sound behind him...

THWHACK!!!

Barton spins, pulls his sidearm, and aims, only to find a hulking brute lying flat on the floor, his gun still in his unconscious hand. Confused at the sight, for a moment, Barton looks up to find the answer to why he is not shot, bleeding, or dying.

"Looks like I am going to get that whupping from momma after all! Doesn't it, Sir?"

Barton breathes a sigh of relief and shakes his head, in disbelief. Standing at the door, with a grin from ear to ear and holding a piece of oak lumber in his hand, is the young livery worker, Isaac.

"Good enough," Barton says simply, but gratefully.

"What you gonna do now Sir?" Isaac inquires, as he checks the prostrate hulk on the floor, still holding the oaken plank in his hand, just in case.

"As soon as I can get Smoke saddled and packed, I am headed for Topeka. There is a good chance that my son is waiting for me there."

Isaac puts the piece of oaken wood across his shoulders, behind his head, holding it there with both hands. His grin grows into one of his signature smiles, as he announces, "Sir, you're going to be starting that trip sooner than you think because that fine horse is standing outside of this very building. He still hasn't been one minute since you left. I thought if I put his saddle and tack on, he would settle down. But, when I got him all cinched up, he kicked open the stall door and got out. I followed him up here. When we heard the gunfire, I figured I had better come to help before that horse did. I ain't never been good with a gun, but I can swing oak planks all day. I just pretended that that fellow was the south end of a northbound bull and laid into him. Did pretty good, didn't I, Sir?"

"You did just fine, young man," Barton replied with a slight grin appearing.

"What you going to do about her, Mr. Anderson?"

Barton, for a moment, had forgotten about Big Bea, who is not quite as mouthy and full of herself, with all of her bruisers dead, or laid out.

"The sheriff, and his eager deputies, are going to be here soon. He will find nothing when he arrives, other than this big ruffian laying on the ground. You will tell the law that he enjoyed the house booze too much, ran into the door, and knocked himself out. As for the dead ones, you will share that they had to leave town, for a family emergency, and are going to be gone a long time. You, and some of your girls, can drag the bodies somewhere the sheriff has never been, in this big house, until this moron wakes up and can haul them off. Do you understand, Ms. Wingmire?"

Knowing that Barton has the best plan to keep her out of trouble with the law, she shakes her head, to the affirmative.

Barton, with Isaac following, makes his way out the back door, where Barton whistles and Smoke arrives in the alley, ready for his range partner to get on and get going.

Barton turns to Isaac, touches his finger to the brim of his hat, and says, "I owe you one, young man."

Isaac, putting his hands on his hips and raring back, answers, "No, Sir! I reckon I have some stories to tell momma, now, about the man from Smithview and his big gray horse!"

Barton nods his head, puts the heels of his boots against Smoke's sides, and they are off for Topeka.

5

The campfire crackles and dances, as Barton stares into it, perhaps hoping to see a vision of what the future holds. He, and his equine companion, have traveled a couple of hours since leaving Lawrence. Barton had been torn between trying to make Topeka without pausing or stopping to rest and eat along the way. Again, he hears the wise words of a U.S. marshal friend, "Do not be in a hurry to make a fatal mistake." So, Smoke is munching on some soft grass and Barton has made a fast meal of beans and jerked meat. The heat from the fire has a therapeutic effect on Barton, causing him to relax and release the encounter with Big Bea and her flunkies. He knows that what is waiting for him, in Topeka, is a far more formidable challenge, one that will take him being at his sharpest, his fastest, and his most hardened.

An hour has passed, Smoke is sleeping with one hind leg relaxed, and Barton has thrown a bedroll and blanket close to the cracking fire. He lays down on his makeshift bed, places his hands behind his head, and looks up at the star-filled Kansas night. He knows that sleep will not come easy, for the number of thoughts, running through his mind, seem to be as numerous as the twinkling lights in the celestial sphere.

For now, Barton can't make an exact plan on how to retrieve Seth and get out of Topeka without anyone knowing. Or, at least, knowing until he has established a retreat that is far enough ahead of any likely reaction and pursuit. He knows that, as he does with his covert vocation, he will get to town, locate the man known as Henry Livingston, and observe any patterns or habits that Barton can take advantage of. He accepts that this will be more than just confronting a mark, killing him, and leaving town. If Livingston is as much of a hard-ass as Bea Wingmire implies that he is, then Barton will not be battling another man's ability to draw a gun. An outlaw is just fighting to live another day, but Barton knows he will be fighting against an ego, a pride, an arrogance that Livingston has relied upon to build a flourishing business empire. An empire that this man of influence will not allow to be touched, nor the perks that come with it, whether it be power, money, lifestyle, or family.

So, Barton will use this time to consider the one thing that he has more control over, or at least he hopes he does. He knows that any future life, on the Anderson ranch, will never be the same, for him or Seth. Barton, sometimes, feels futile when he considers the unfortunate things that will have to be explained to his youngest boy. Things like where his mom, brother, and grandfather are? Why they will no longer be in his life? Barton doesn't know how much Seth saw that morning when the Ford gang brought devastation to their home. But Barton and Jenny always taught the boys to be honest, no matter how much they think it might hurt or make someone uncomfortable. When those questions come, he hopes that there is enough 'fatherhood' still left in him to meet this daunting challenge.

Another thing, that keeps swelling up in Barton's senses, is the status of the relationship between him and his son. Will Seth be able to comprehend what his father is now? Can a seven-year-old grasp what Barton has to do to stay out of prison? Will Seth be able to perceive the risks that are presented to anyone who appears to be of value to a man who has left a trail of death behind him, legal or not? Will Seth be able to accept why he can live at the ranch, with Jeff and Sally, but Barton chooses not to? Can Seth grow up, grounded and blooming, with a father that sends for him, and then sends him away, for his protection? As much as Barton realizes that this 'arm's length' parenting is not perfect, he knows that it is not negotiable.

And there is another consideration that Barton dismisses quickly, but deep in his reasoning, he knows it could present itself, no matter how miniscule the odds are of it becoming a reality. What if Seth does not want to go back to Smithview? What if he has such a grand life, with the Livingstons, that he has embraced it and he knows that 'life as usual' is gone from him on the ranch? This development will never be accepted by Barton, because he will not allow his son to be raised by the tyrannical soul that Henry Livingston seems to be. To the death, Barton will never surrender his boy to such an upbringing.

Barton closes his eyes and goes to sleep, for the morning will come quickly.

It was after twelve noon when Barton and Smoke rode into Topeka. The lunch bustle, the normal activities of daily life, and the people who are in town for government business make it easy for them to not be noticed, unlike a smaller town like Prestonburg or Smithview. If Barton was looking for a fugitive, then he would hit the popular saloons and gambling houses, places where a man on the run would spend their newfound bounty. But with Livingston, the gathering of vital information will have to be performed at the places that that type of man would frequent, such as banks, post offices, lawyers, etc. As much as Barton wanted to find Seth and take him home, he knew this was going to take time and diligence, to get the proper results that he wanted, and needed.

Barton worked his way around the city, initially getting little knowledge of this man named Henry Livingston. He tried to be unpretentious about how he approached those who might know something. The responses, that Barton perceived, were imbedded in three truths: the person had heard of Livingston but didn't know anything, the person knew Livingston but was wary of sharing information with a stranger, or the person knew Livingston and was afraid to share anything that might get back to this ruthless figure. When it looked like he would never get a foot in the evasive door of Livingston's kingdom, fate decided to dance with opportunity, and Barton was presented with a golden way to go inside the world of Henry Livingston.

Barton, upon spotting a sign that advertised a shipping company, decided to go in and make conversation, maybe even see if they knew Arnie Proffitt, the cargo hauler of Smithview. Once he walked upon the loading platform, it didn't take long for a conversation to be initiated.

"Hey, big man, can I be of help to you?" a voice came from behind Barton.

When he turned, to acknowledge the salutation, Barton discovered the voice belonged to a muscular man with a long beard, overalls, and a friendly smile.

"Oh, I am in town on shipping business, and I am just passing the time until I go to my appointment. Just was interested in what kind of operation you ran here," Barton responds.

The big gentleman walks over to Barton, extends a large hand that is attached to an arm that is as big as most men's legs, and says, "I am Rand Cannon. I own this business that you wish to inspect. You say you are in the shipping business too?"

Barton, playing his cards close to the vest, answers, "No, not in the business, just here on business for a friend of mine in Smithview. You might know him, Arnie Proffitt?"

Rand runs his hand over his beard, looks up for a moment, in a pose of contemplation, then remarks, "No, I don't know of him, personally. I have heard of him, have seen a few of his cargo wagons around the area. But I have never met him. What business could you have in Topeka, for a shipper in Smithview?"

Barton, sensing that Rand might be feeling threatened that another cargo company might be moving in on his area, is quick to put the brawny man at ease.

"Oh, I am just here for Arnie. He heard that I was going to the state capitol. I guess some big trader, with interests around Smithview, had forgotten to pay a bill for some freight that Arnie picked up for him. I just need to find him, hand him the bill, and remind him that business keeps moving when the money keeps coming in. That's all I am here for."

Rand, looking more at ease with his new acquaintance, asks to see the bill so that he can help Barton locate the merchant. With quick thinking, knowing there is no such bill of laden, Barton lifts his hands and shakes them, in a negative manner.

"Sorry, but I get the feeling that this might not have been a transaction that will be recorded in the open books, if you know what I mean. I guess extra money was paid to "not know too much", so I better stay with the plan, which is to deliver the charges and don't look at them or talk about them."

Rand laughs, winks, and elbows Barton with a force that knocks him back a step.

"I have had a few of those deals myself, cowboy. I understand what you are saying. That's the extra money that buys the wife something pretty and nice, the kids something new, or keeps the whiskey bottle fresh in my office, in there. You can, at least, tell me who is getting this bill, so I can help a fellow shipper on his way, right?"

Barton, quickly, responds, "Some guy named Henry Livingston. I guess he is a big wheel up here. I haven't ever heard of him, have you, Mr. Cannon?"

Instantly, the smile disappears from the burly man's face, replaced by a sullen demeanor. Barton is now concerned that this well of possibilities has dried up as quickly as it opened.

"Mr. Henry Livingston, you say? We call him 'Sixty Days Livingston' around here. As in, you haul anything for him, you won't be seeing your freight fees for, at least, sixty days. I get so mad I could bite a nail in two, but he does a lot of lucrative business with us. He just takes his own blame time in paying for the services."

Barton, feeling relieved that the conversation is still alive, takes a chance and asks if Rand can tell him where Livingston could be found.

"Better than that, cowboy," Rand replies. "I have a wagon going to his house today, delivering some piece of fancy European furniture. It came in on the train yesterday and I want to get it out of here before someone scratches it and we catch hell for 'damaging its ambiance', whatever that is."

Barton feels a sense of hope rising in him, with the first solid information he has retrieved since he got to Topeka. But, as fast as he is given real anticipation of locating Seth, his prospects are dashed with Rand's next words.

"Oh, wait a minute. It's a two-man job, and one of my haulers is out today, dropped a farm plow on his foot yesterday, and he is now hopping around like a horny rooster. Sorry, cowboy. It will be a few days before we will be gracing the Livingston estate with our attendance. I guess I will just have to worry about that blasted fancy cabinet until then."

Barton's mind is racing, he could have used the shipping wagon as cover, at least to get to the main gate. Then, an idea hits him that will get him to the entrance, and possibly into the estate.

"Here's a thought, I don't know if you would be open to it. If you really want to get that expensive headache out of here, and you need two men to deliver it, how about I volunteer to help? Seeing that I am going that way, I will ride along with your driver, and give him a hand. Once we get your job done, I will just hand someone my bill and we will be out of there. Sounds pretty slick, to me."

Rand is shaking his head, in the affirmative, as Barton shares his sudden idea. Then, the cargo man turns and yells for his driver to come out where the two men are standing. A short stocky man appears from the warehouse, reaching out his hand. While shaking the tall man's hand, the worker introduces himself as Wilbur, and then asks the visitor for his.

"Andy is my name", Barton answers. "Nice to meet you, Wilbur. Let's get that choice piece of furniture loaded, I'll tie my horse to your wagon, and we can get this thing delivered before the sun goes down."

After thirty minutes of loading and hauling, the wagon pulls in front of their final destination, the Livingston estate. The first thing that Barton notices is the granite stone wall that surrounds the property, enhanced by two large metal gates in the front. Barton hopes that his plan, going in with the wagon, will be productive. It is plain to see that getting in, any other way, would be nearly impossible. And, if he does get in, getting out may pose the same suspect odds of success.

"We are here to deliver that European unit to the Livingstons," Wilbur announces as two armed guards come and look under the canvas that is covering the load.

"Who is he?" one of the men asks, pointing at Barton.

"This is Andy. He is a guy that the boss got to help. Redd dropped a farm plow on his foot, and he is going to milk that for as long as he can. You know how ornery Redd can be when it comes to hard work," Wilbur chuckles, as another armed sentry joins them.

The first guard continues to stare at Barton, then asks, "Don't I know you from somewhere? You look familiar."

Barton's heartbeat gets quicker at the thought of Seth being on the other side of this wall. But his plan of entrance may be coming undone, and his effort may be set back to who knows when and where.

"No, I don't think so. I have never been to Topeka before. I am just here helping out. Can't wait to get out of here and get back on the road, "Barton calmly explains.

After looking under the canvas cover, the second guard walks around the wagon and looks at Smoke, who is tied to the wagon and is standing quietly, for now.

"What is the horse for?" the sentry asks, still looking the big gray horse over.

Barton responds, "He is blind. When we get done here, I am supposed to take him to an animal doctor who has a reputation for knowing about things like that. If he can't help the horse, I have been ordered to take him outside of town, someplace where no one will notice, and shoot him."

Smoke, upon hearing this, jerks his head up and looks at Barton. While he is not capable of understanding the English language, he has heard the words 'horse' and 'shoot' enough to get his attention. Barton holds his breath, hoping that Smoke doesn't snap his lead line and make a break for it.

The lead guard waves for the furniture wagon to enter through the large gates, looks up at Barton, and says, "If the horse doctor can't help, there is a soap factory outside of Topeka. They not only will put this miserable plug out of its misery, but they might give you a dollar or two for him."

Barton just keeps looking forward, trying to calm the feeling to shoot the dotish guard, in an effort to put him out of his misery of being so stupid. Plus, Barton doesn't have any desire to look back at Smoke, in fear that his equine friend may discern more than any of them can imagine.

Once the furniture wagon is directed to a side entrance, where they will unload and carry the piece of expensive furniture into the desired location, they are met by a regally dressed black man, probably sixty years old or so.

"My name is Jeremiah Jensen, I am the head butler of the Livingston estate. I will lead you to the room where Ms. Livingston would like the new armoire to be placed. You will have to go up three ascending flights of stairs, so be prepared for that. Rest if you need to, but not for long. The master of the house does not like for strangers to linger on the property."

Barton, already, sees that this is not a place for his youngest son and that the so-called 'master of the house' is a horse's ass that has no business raising any kid, let alone his.

After attempting to put the wagon as close to the door as possible, Wilbur pulls back on the reins and yells 'Whoa'! Barton quickly jumps down and walks to the back of the wagon. There he unties Smoke and utters the only three words that will be needed in this situation.

"Stay close, Smoke."

Wilbur starts removing the canvas cover from over the expensive unit of fine furniture. With Jeremiah watching every move, Wilbur and Barton grab each end of the French armoire and head toward the door. As he walks to the entrance, Barton looks up at the enormous residence that they are about to enter. It is plain to see that it is a three-story structure, sided with the same granite stone that the property wall is made of. Barton surmises that each floor has a purpose. The first would be for public affairs and parties, the second for more private gatherings and family relaxation, and the third was the private living quarters for the family. Somehow, if this piece of furniture does not wind up on the third floor, then he will have to devise a way for that to happen. Barton can feel something inside telling him that that is where a sign of Seth can be found.

"Be careful! Be careful with the door frame, please!"

This would be Jeremiah's narrative the entire time that Barton, and Wilbur, are transporting the expensive cabinet to its destination. Barton notices that Wilbur is getting winded, and they haven't even made it up the first flight of steps. If they have to go further, he is concerned if his moving partner is going to make it. Then, a cruel thought crosses Barton's mind, that a well-timed heart attack, by Wilbur, might present Barton with the necessary cover he would need. But he lets that consideration pass and tries to keep Wilbur, and the heavy cabinet, moving in an upward direction.

"Keep moving, gentlemen. Keep moving, only one more flight of stairs and you will be there," was the urging of the head butler.

When they finally reached the third floor, Jeremiah directed them to place the armoire in the first door on the left. Wilbur kept pleading to set the load down and rest, only to be reminded that it was just a little further and they could put it down for good. Barton knows that when they put the cabinet in its final place, his true purpose is only beginning.

But it would seem that fate would, again, be with the searching father on this day. As they entered the room, it was plain to see that this was a bedroom where a young person would stay. Barton looked around the expanse, while he had the opportunity, searching for any sign that this was where a young boy lives. The bed, the chair, the desk could be used by a seven-year-old, but there wasn't one telltale sign, of his son. Until Barton saw it, and his knees went weak upon the sight of it.

A large painting of Seth on the wall.

Getting a grip on his mind, Barton stood and gazed at the picture of the handsome smiling boy, hanging in a cherrywood frame. He had to study it for a bit, understanding that his son was, now, a year older than the last time he saw him, his hair was longer, he was dressed in finery that was not normal in ranch life, and that the artist had, probably, taken some license with his interpretation of his subject. But there was no doubt, that was Seth.

"Sir, your task is done, you need to leave the premises, immediately," Jeremiah ordered.

"That is a fine-looking boy, where is he today?"

"Well, sir, that is none of your business, none at all, "Jeremiah responded, as he walked over to an ornate cord, coming out of the wall, and jerked on it repeatedly. Within moments, they were joined by six sturdy-looking men, armed with rifles, batons, and a rope.

"There is no reason to get all serious about a simple question about the boy on the wall. Just a good-looking young man that might be worth meeting," was Barton's reply. Wilbur, feeling a growing tension, slips out of the room.

"It will be a cold day in hell before you ever meet my son, Andy. Or should I say, Anderson," another voice now enters into the scenario. In a joined effort, the hulking group of men step aside, and a dapperly dressed man steps into the room. By the reactions of the butler and the heavies, Barton assumes that this is the master of the house, Henry Livingston, himself.

Smiling confidently, Livingston continues, "I don't know what you did to piss off the queen whore in Lawrence, but I just received a telegram from her, warning me of your arrival. From all the colorful words she included in it, it probably cost her a fortune to send it. Yep, she is one very mad madam."

Barton, realizing that he is outmanned, outgunned, and out of options, makes his play, realizing he has nothing to lose now.

"There is just one problem with that, Mr. Livingston. He is not your son, he is mine. And I am here to take him home or die trying. You know I am telling the truth, and the boy knows it too. He may be a current resident in your house, but he will never be your son. He has Anderson blood running through him, and it will rise to the top, today or someday. So, do the right thing, and let me have Seth and I am gone."

Livingston smirks, and shakes his head, as in amazement at Barton's statement. Then, a serious look comes over the well-groomed face as he raises his voice, while he points his finger at the tall man before him.

"His name is not Seth, it is Jackson Livingston. He is my son because I have the paperwork, the lawyers, and the judges that will proclaim that he is my son. Here is your problem, you trail trash. You come here with two options, and leaving here with your boy is not going to be something that happens today, so I guess all you have left to do is die!"

Livingston raises his hand, and snaps his fingers, and the six henchmen rush Barton with a vicious force. Although he gets in a few good punches and kicks, eventually Barton is overwhelmed and taken down to the floor. The onslaught of baton strikes and kicks is relentless. Barton, frantically, spits blood from his mouth, trying to find a way to keep breathing, which is further hindered by the pain from the broken ribs that continue to be abused by the ruffians. Barton starts losing his sight, whether because of his fleeting consciousness or by his eyes swelling closed, from the pummeling that his face continues to receive.

Then, the attack stops. Barton wonders if there has been a change of thought from his attackers. When he, finally, gets one eye open enough to see, he observes Henry Livingston standing over him. The rich tycoon bends over his fallen visitor and in a last act of disrespect, whispers, "Hey, you miserable son-of-a-bitch, no one comes into my house and takes anything. And, to shove a last stab into your dying heart, the boy isn't even here. He is in Europe with his new momma. You did this for nothing. Goodbye, Mr. Anderson! I will be sure to tell Jackson that you were sorry to have missed him."

And with that, the last thing that Barton will experience is the sight of the heel of an expensive Italian shoe headed for his face.

Nothing, now, but darkness and silence, for consciousness has left the fallen cowboy.

6

———————

"Can you hear me, Andy? Are you alive, cowboy?"

Those were the first words that Barton discerned as his consciousness grappled to awaken in him. Trying as desperately as he could, he could not get his sight to return, simply hearing the inquiring words, of a nearby voice, in his dark circumstances. Strangely, it seemed to be a voice that he thought he knew, but clear comprehension was fleeting, as his cognizance wavered, in and out.

"Just lay easy, Andy. You are hurt really bad, I don't know how bad. I don't dare send for a doctor, not knowing if the sawbones is a drinking friend of Henry Livingston. We are just going to have to do the best we can and pray that you are strong enough to recover from the thrashing that Livingston's men put on you."

Barton, still fighting for some sort of comprehension of where he was and who he was with, is frustrated by his lack of sight. He lifts his right hand up to his swollen face and waves it weakly, trying to observe anything, even a shadow, that would affirm that this obscurity is fading.

"You can forget seeing anything, at least for a day or two. Your eyes are swelled shut tighter than a newborn kitten's. Cowboy, there isn't much on you that hasn't been waylaid by Livingston's crew. I ain't a doctor, but I would say that whatever isn't bleeding, bruised, or broken hasn't had a chance to show it yet."

Barton reaches out, in the direction of the solicitous voice, and finds a face that is attached to a long, silky beard. Barton, in a moment of recognition, starts to realize who this person is, that is showing compassion upon his situation.

"That's right, Andy. This is Rand Cannon. You just rest and try to get some healing started. Don't worry. You are in a safe place, an old, abandoned warehouse that Livingston's men can't find. Only Wilber and I know you are here, and he is too scared to show his face outside. When you have recovered some of your strength and awareness, we will have time to talk about what your situation is and how you got here. But, for now, just lay back and try to sleep."

Unable to resist or respond otherwise, Barton lays his hand by his side and falls into a deep slumber.

It would be almost thirty-six hours before Barton would find another state of consciousness that allowed him to, at least, hear Rand and Wilbur as they encouraged the injured stranger to just lay quiet and not worry. As Barton awoke from his dormancy, which protected him from feeling how bad his injuries were, his tolerance for pain was driven to its limits as consciousness came back. Realizing that Barton was in excruciating discomfort, Wilbur said that a shot of corn whiskey would help bring some relief, but the cowboy shook his head no. It was as if he wanted to remember every twinge of torture that his body was experiencing, to not forget any of it when it was time for those to pay for it.

"Here, Andy, it ain't much, but you haven't eaten in two days, and you ain't going to heal unless we get some sustenance into you," Wilber pleaded, holding the awaiting spoon up to Barton's mouth.

Initially, Barton hesitates to take on the liquid fare, knowing that every muscle needed to move the soup along has been beaten and abused, especially in his mid-section. But, once the gumbo-like concoction found its destination, the perception of hunger was awakened and Barton was ready for the second, third, and the following helpings. For now, provision over pain was the order of the moment.

On the third morning of Barton being in this secret shelter, he woke up to the reality of sight in his right eye. As he felt his face, he could tell that the swelling was going down and the throbbing pain was not as severe. Upon getting some focus in his vision, he looked around his current primitive sanctuary. It appeared to be a very rough storage room that was not used very much and had been forgotten until the need for a safe haven presented itself. The accumulation of dust, and the clusters of cobwebs, gave the impression that this was where he needed to be, at least for now.

"Sorry about the accommodations, cowboy," the husky hauler laughed, as he brought another bowl of simple pottage to the awaiting patient. "I guess we could have put you up in the Topeka Ritz, but seeing that a certain businessman, with a real dislike for you, owns it, this will have to do."

Barton, with help from Rand, sets up in his makeshift cot and prepares to satisfy his growling stomach. Rand is glad to see that Barton's appetite is growing, as that is the only means of treating Barton's injuries, without getting an outside physician involved in the situation. Having been a businessman in Topeka for a few years, Rand understands how the elite cultural circles work, and they can be willing to sell their souls to rise up a notch on the social ladder, especially if it gets them in tighter with a man like Henry Livingston.

"How did I get here?" Barton asks, in between helpings of stew. "The last thing I remember is being rushed by Livingston's men, in the big house."

Rand pulls a box over by where Barton is propped up and sits down. The cargo man knows this tale is going to take a while to tell, and may have to be told in multiple installments if Barton needs to rest.

"Wilbur came running and yelling into the loading dock, acting like a crazy man. I liked to have never got him to calm down. He told me about what was happening up at the Livingston house, how they were giving you an overall stomping. When I asked him why, he said that you told Livingston that the boy he has is really yours. Is that true, Andy? Is that kid, that the Livingstons showed up with about a year ago, really your son?"

Barton, groaning from the pain as he repositions himself on his bed, answers, "Yes, he is my son. He was taken from my ranch by outlaw scum. Then, he was sold to the Livingstons by a whore in Lawrence. His name is Seth, and when I get healed up, I will go up there, get him, and I will kill them all the next time. Any future encounters will be on my terms and the odds will be in my favor. My mistake almost cost me my life, and for now, the return of my son."

Rand reaches over, takes the empty bowl and spoon from Barton, and then shares a surprising observation. "Well, as far as they are concerned, you are dead!"

When Barton turns his head, in a sign of not understanding, Rand tells of how he and Wilbur went to the Livingston estate, not knowing how they could be of help. After sitting, and watching for an hour, they noticed a small supply wagon coming out of the front gates. Two large men were sitting in the seat, with something wrapped in a canvas tarp in the back. After realizing that the tarp was the cargo cover that he had put on the expensive furniture, Rand said he played a hunch, hoping he might be right. He and Wilbur, now riding horses, would follow the wagon, trying not to be noticed. Once the Livingston men got outside the city limits, they stopped at a vacant field, dug a large hole, tossed the canvas-wrapped item into the hole, and covered it up. Finally, they loaded up their shovels and drove away toward town. Rand, suddenly, gets an edge to his voice, as he recalls that they were laughing, like it was some kind of game to them.

Barton, sitting up straighter, gets an enraged look on his face, as he says, "They laughed after they buried a man alive?"

Rand, seeing that Barton is expending too much energy, for the condition he is in, coaxes his visitor to lay back down and then shares a truth that may be the terms that Barton talked about, when he goes back for Seth.

"Hang on a minute, before you have a setback. They weren't laughing because they had buried a man alive, but were laughing because they thought you were dead, and you wouldn't be any more trouble to them. This may be the 'Ace-in-the-hole' that you were looking for. They have no idea that you are still alive, are still planning on getting your son, and they will have their guards down when you do come. Think about it, cowboy."

Barton closes his one good eye, for a moment, until he gets a perplexed look on his face, turns to his caretaker, and asks, "If they didn't know I wasn't dead, you didn't either, did you?"

Rand, leaning back on the old shipping box he is sitting on, lets out a hearty laugh, and continues, "Scared the hell out of Wilber, I am telling you! We got over there, dug you up with our bare hands. We loaded your body on the back of a horse, intending to take it to the U.S. Marshal's office. But all of a sudden, you groaned under the canvas cover. I thought Wilbur was going to crap his pants. I just knew that my cargo partner was two breaths away from needing that empty grave, himself!"

Wanting to chuckle at Rand's storytelling, but knowing it would hurt too much, he places his hands on his sides and is content to just sigh his approval. Then, Barton turns to Rand, with a look of concern moving over his face, and asks, "Aren't you afraid of Livingston coming after you? When he gets wind of this, he is going to be pretty mad and will want retribution."

"That is the beauty of our situation," Rand starts. "He doesn't have a clue that you are alive, who rescued you, nothing. He is sitting on his royal rear end, up there in that mansion, thinking all is well in his kingdom. As far as he is concerned, the king of the Livingston estate has won again. He doesn't have any idea that a hurt storm is coming his way, and he is going to think he sat 'bare-assed on a rabid porcupine' when you get through with him!"

Barton lays still, rubbing his good eye with his right hand, trying to take in everything that he has been told in the last few minutes. Rand, sensing a change in the mindset of his patient, gets up, and says, "Time for another bowl of Wilbur's award-winning soup. We have got to get you up because there is a young man waiting for his daddy to show up, I just know it. Ain't that right, Andy? Or should I say, Anderson?"

Barton, trying to discern what this revelation might mean, lifts his hand up and reaches toward the cargo man. Rand takes Barton's hand, gently holds it, and then shares that if all works out well, the next hand to touch the tall man's will be the small hand of a young man named Seth. Barton nods, in agreement.

Another few days pass, and the care for Barton continues. Cuts are treated, bruises are given an application of a liniment that is used on racehorses with muscle trauma, and Wilber took some old cottonseed sacks to make a wrap for Barton's cracked ribs. While he is not yet ready to go after Seth again, things are more improved than when his shipping friends dug him from a fresh grave and brought him to this isolated warehouse room.

Barton was finishing up his first bowl of gumbo for the day, when Wilber came running into the hideaway, looking like he had seen a ghost or some other outlandish personality. When Rand, finally gets him to settle down enough to speak in distinguishable words, the shaken dockworker announces that someone was at the shipping office, and they were asking if Wilbur had seen a stranger around the dock, a tall man riding a big gray horse.

Barton, sitting up in his makeshift stretcher bed, waved for Wilbur to come closer to him, as his sight was not fully rehabilitated.

"Have you ever seen him before? Did he say who he was? Could he be here snooping around for Livingston?" Barton quizzes, knowing that he is not ready for a physical confrontation with anyone, at this point.

Wilbur, still shaking from anxiety, answers, "I haven't ever seen this guy before, and I know a lot of people around here. He didn't seem to be too excited about locating you, just asking if I had seen anyone that would match that description. Do you think he is a Livingston man? Oh, my Lord, have they found us? Are we going to die?"

Barton, concerned about any person asking questions, even if they are general in nature, knows he needs to ply Wilber's mind for any information that has not made itself available among Wilbur's ramblings.

"Is there anything else about this stranger that might be helpful in knowing his intentions or who he might be here representing?"

The shaking dockworker thinks for a minute, makes a face

that would give the impression he is in deep thought, and then blurts out.

"Oh, yeah! He was wearing a badge and said he was a U.S. marshal!"

Rand takes a couple of steps, in Wilbur's direction, and yells," Damn, Wilbur! At what point in your dang report do you think it would have been, slightly, important to share that bit of information? A federal lawman is asking about a man that we are hiding, and you just let that part slip your mind? Sometimes, you amaze me!"

Barton is not amazed, as much as he is invested in the possibility of this being who he thinks it is, and hopes that it is.

"Did he say what his name was? What did he look like? Did he say any more?"

Wilbur, disappointed that he has not been able to bring news that would make them glad to have him on the job, says, "I don't remember if he said his name or not. I was so blame nervous and didn't want to slip up and say anything I shouldn't. I don't remember if he said his name. I just remember that he was older than you, not as tall as you, and his horse's name was Hickory."

Barton knows who the inquisitive stranger is, as he slowly lets out a breath and allows his mind to consider what this means, that this may be the best news he could receive, on this day.

"Rand, go find him," Barton urges. "His name is Lyndon Tomes, he is a U.S. marshal and can be trusted. He may be the only friend that we have, or at least know of, in Topeka. Just tell him that you know where the man is that he is asking about. Then, tell him to wait for further word from you. I trust him. I just need to know why he is looking for me and what he knows."

After Rand leaves, Barton lies back down and tries to perceive what Tomes' arrival means to the current situation of things. If it were just going after bandits and fugitives, it would be a simple operation of finding and confronting. But, if Barton has learned anything, from his first encounter with Henry Livingston, it's that all of the methods of performing duties, as the Janitor, can be thrown out the window. All he needs is to find one weakness, one chink in the rich man's armor, and exploit it. Then Barton will have that edge that he didn't have at the Livingston estate. And, once the flaw in the Livingston kingdom is found, will Tomes be able to go through it with Barton, or will he be bound by the oath of a lawman? 'Hell or high water' will have to be the mindset when the chance to retrieve Seth presents itself.

Then, in the midst of all of these new considerations coming into his mind, Barton has a new matter rise up to contemplate, one that he is surprised that it has taken so long to manifest itself.

Where is Smoke? What has happened to his equine friend?

Barton's pondering of the status of Smoke is interrupted when Rand comes into the room. The shipping owner tells Barton that he found the marshal about five blocks away. The lawman was heading back to the main part of the business district and had stopped to check the cinch on his saddle. Without drawing attention to either one of them, Rand pulled his horse up to a nearby watering trough. While Rand's ride was drinking, he told Tomes to keep looking at his saddle and his chestnut horse. Tomes was instructed to stay in this location. If the man, that the marshal was asking about, wanted to see him, then Rand would return. When the lawman saw him, Tomes was not to acknowledge him, just get on Hickory and follow him, from a safe distance.

Once they got to a safe place, further instructions would be given on how to find this tall man that the marshal seemed to need to find.

"So, do I go back and what do I tell him?" asked Rand, with Barton sitting on the side of the bed now.

"Once he follows you back here, tell him I don't need his badge, I need his gun. If he can't fill that bill, then keep on riding. I am not concerned about being law-abiding, I am concerned about getting my son back," was Barton's reply, as he reaches over to where Rand has laid his Colt pistol, which the cargo man had retrieved from Barton's temporary grave. He pulls the revolver out of its holster, rolling it around in his hand to test if it felt right.

Once Rand had left, to go retrieve the marshal, Barton stood up. It had been days since he had been in a vertical position, and his legs were not sure that this was a stable position that could be maintained, for long. Wilbur watched, ready to leap to Barton's assistance if it looked like Barton's fight to stay upright was starting to fade. Barton put his gun belt on, slid the sidearm out of its holder, then back into the leather holster. For almost an hour, this was an action that he repeated, over and over, trying to get his reflexes to come to life, after being dormant for so long. He kept at it, repeatedly, until he heard a voice that he had not heard since Prestonsburg when they were both standing over the body of Coy Newton.

"I have seen buffalo carcasses that look better than you, gunslinger!"

"What took you so long, lawman?" Barton asked, without turning to acknowledge the entrance of Tomes.

"You are a hard man to trail, seeing that you don't talk to anyone, you don't ever tell anyone what you are doing. So to find you, I have to follow the trail of dead bodies and angry whores, hoping someone saw the 'tall man on the big gray horse' before you get ambushed or worse. And may I comment on the fact that if you were a cat, you wouldn't have too many lives left!"

Barton continues to perform the ritual of drawing his gun,

putting it back, then removing it again. While he is not at his fastest or surest, he is getting better, and the natural instincts are returning.

"Did the husky, bearded man tell you that if you are coming as a lawman, then stay out of my way? The law has no place in what I am getting ready to do, and you don't either. Keep riding and take your shiny badge with you."

Tomes instructs Barton to turn around. When Barton does, the marshal has a smirk on his face, that slowly grows into a smile, Tomes says, simply, "It's time to take Seth home."

Barton has never seen this look on the U.S. Marshal's face. He looks Tomes in the eyes and sharply proclaims, "I don't know what you are grinning about. It's going to get ugly, Tomes. People are going to die, a lot of people are going to die. One of us may not come out of this unmarked. Both of us may wind up six feet under, in a pine box. Senator Richards can't get us out of what's getting ready to happen. There is no other way for me to get my son back, but to take him."

"Sir, I believe you are greatly mistaken in your assessment of the situation. I think there might just be another way for you to see your son again," comes the sound of another voice.

When they all turn around, they discover the dialogue is coming from an elderly black man, sixty years old or so, dressed in a very nice livery suit. It is Jeremiah Jenson, the head butler that they had met at Henry Livingston's house.

Whether it was shock, confusion, or fatigue that was overcoming him, Barton did his best to walk over to the old man, still dressed in his immaculate uniform for work.

"You have got a hell of a lot of nerve coming here. I don't know how you found your way here and don't care. I just know that we can't let you leave, go tell Livingston that I am alive, that I am coming after my son, and to kill that pompous bastard."

Jeremiah looks at the other men in the room, then looks

back at Barton, and replies, "I think it would be advantageous of you, sir, if you quit wasting your energy on making futile plans that have no chance of being successful. Or have you forgotten the last time you invited yourself to the Livingston estate? I would suggest you enlist these men to help you prepare to leave Topeka and get away as fast, and as far, as you can. It would be rather wise to leave before Mr. Livingston finds out the truth that the one, we call Jackson, is not there. Oh, you were told that young Livingston was in Europe, but that was not exactly the truth."

Barton, feeling his strength starting to slip from him, takes a big breath, and attempts to refocus his attention. When he feels he has more control of his senses, he asks, "I don't understand you, old man. If the one you call Jackson, whose real name is Seth, is not in Europe and is not in that big house, then where in the hell is he?"

Jeremiah says nothing, just stands still for a moment. Then he, calmly, takes two steps sideways, revealing that there is yet another person in the room. Barton has to look twice, to make sure he isn't having a hallucination from his injuries. But even though the individual looked a year older, his hair is longer, and he is dressed finer than any time on the ranch, Barton realized that who was standing by Jeremiah wasn't a hallucination or a dream.

It was Seth.

7

"Daddy, is that you?"

Shock can do mysterious things to the human mind. It can disable the mental capabilities, unhinge the physical abilities, and make the heart unable to process the raging emotions. And for a few seconds, the visual jolt of the moment has left everyone speechless and motionless.

A young child is shocked by the sight of a rough-looking man he once knew as father.

A father is shocked by seeing the last remaining twig of his family tree.

A lawman is shocked by the reality of a reunion, that he had hoped for, actually happening.

Two strangers are shocked that a common housekeeper could find their hiding place.

"Yes, Son. It is me," responded Barton, feeling the strength in his legs leaving, as the unexpected development of seeing Seth is more than he can handle, due to his condition.

Tomes and Rand, quickly and carefully, grab Barton on each

side and escort him back to the makeshift bed, where Barton can sit down, before he collapses.

While Seth's eyes are not immediately convinced that this is the man who raised him on the Anderson ranch, his young heart is quickly won over. He runs to Barton, throws himself at the tall man, in anticipation of being caught like so many times before. Once the paternal embrace offers a sure haven of safety, the young child's shock gives way to the only appropriate response, in this moment.

Seth cries, uncontrollably.

Barton, summoning up all the might that he can, holds his son tightly. It has been a long time since that barbarous morning on the ranch, that dreadful day in Dog Creek, the tough day of the trial, and the moment of vindication when he confronted Coy Newton in Prestonburg. Barton had forgotten the personal perception of having something to live for and not just having dying as the only option for anything you do, and being compliant with that result.

Barton, still holding Seth against his aching chest, looks around the room, waiting for someone to explain what has just happened. When no word is given or explanation supplied, he looks at the elderly houseman and asks, "Why?"

Jeremiah, shaking his silver-haired head slowly, replies, "I have worked for two generations of Livingstons. I have watched as each one became more selfish, more indifferent, and more willing to cause others the loss that they might have gain. For years, I said nothing, my silence allowing them to corrupt and pillage innocent people, ruining families and lives to keep their ravenous appetites for the 'good life' fed. But, when I watched a man severely beaten, and supposedly killed because he just wanted his son back, that was the final straw. Let's say that hit too close to home. You see, I was taken from my family when I was three. I was sold to a rich, powerful family, not to be an heir, but to be a lifelong servant. And there I remain today. I have too many days behind me to worry about my future, but I cannot let young Jackson here, or Seth as you call him, grow up to be another unprincipled generation of blood-sucking, life-destroying Livingstons. Simple as that, sir."

"But, how did you know that I was still alive? You weren't there when they buried me in that field or when Rand and Wilbur retrieved me," Barton inquires, steadying himself on his elbow as he awaits an answer.

"Mr. Livingston can be counted on to spare no expense when it comes to lifestyle, but he is a pinchfist when it comes to what quality of henchmen he hires," the stately old gentleman says. "The buffoons that do his dirty work are not the smartest, despite their brutish sizes. The two, that were assigned to finish you off, went back to the site of your premature burial because one thought he had dropped a valuable knife there. When they saw that the impromptu grave was empty, they panicked. I overheard them telling another estate guard of the foreboding situation. They saddled their horses and lit out the next morning, aware that they would meet a fate more dire than yours when Mr. Livingston found out what an insufficient job they had done with the real father of Jackson."

Barton's head is spinning, from the ever-changing status of his life, the ever-weakening status of his stamina, to the anticipation of what else could happen on this day.

Marshal Tomes walks over and kneels down by where Barton is sitting on the primitive cot. Still with that slight smirk on his face, finding delight in catching his tall friend by surprise, the lawman continues the explanation of Seth's unexpected appearance at Barton's secret sanctuary.

"It's funny you would mention Jim Richards", the marshal starts. "For the last two days, the senator has been the one who has been managing this developing saga. Seems that Jim's kids go to the same private school that Seth does. Mr. Jensen met the Senator at various school events and developed a trust in him. When he made the decision to right the wrong that had been perpetrated at the Livingston estate, Mr. Jensen approached Jim at a school recital, the day before yesterday, and shared what he had witnessed. Jim, after hearing the description of a 'strapping man with a surly disposition', knew it was you and contacted me. I am in Topeka to be a witness in a range war skirmish. Mr. Jensen, the senator, and I met up yesterday, and arraigned a plan of how to get Seth away from school, and the rest of the story is standing in front of you."

"But, how did you find me here, no one is supposed to know of this place?" Barton inquires, still trying to make sense of how this has come together so quickly, so quietly.

Tomes points at Wilbur, then says, "Once Mr. Jensen shared of your being a part of hauling furniture to the Livingston estate, it was just a matter of time before that one, over there, let down his guard to where I could locate which shipping company. I just watched him as he delivered the type of food that an injured person would need, and followed him. The big one just confirmed what I had already surmised when he brought your message to me."

Barton turns and gives Wilbur a look that could freeze time in its place. Rand slaps the back of the stocky dockworker's head, and utters, "Wilbur, you truly never cease to amaze me."

Suddenly, Barton is made aware of something that has been happening while the men are discussing the particulars of how this gathering has taken place. Seth has been taking a nearby cloth, daubed with liniment, and has been attending to the various bruises and wounds that his father still has. Barton lowers his face, where he is looking Seth in the eyes, and softly speaks to his youngest, "Be patient with me. This is going to take some getting used to."

Barton turns to Tomes, and says, "It seems that we have averted a confrontation. But I can't believe that this is going to culminate with Seth and I leaving Topeka without some repercussions from Livingston. Am I right, Mr. Jensen?"

"Oh, how I wish that you and the young lad could just ride off and renew your family ties," the old man responds. "Once the master, of the Livingston house, discovers what has happened, right under his contemptuous nose, he will tear Topeka apart looking for those who played a part in this brazen endeavor. I cannot return to the estate, that is for sure, as my life is now as worthless as a Confederate coin. And, when he finds out that you, Mr. Anderson, are alive, well, it will become more imperative that your departure be as soon as possible. I have seen Mr. Livingston's unconstrained rage rise up like a prairie fire being nurtured by a stiff western wind. Nothing is safe or sacred when Master Henry's sanity is impaired by his egotistical sense of grandeur.

Barton, continuing to be ministered to by the caring hands of Seth, takes on a look of mystery and states, "In the short time I endured your former boss, he never struck me as one who was graced with great paternal instincts."

"Has nothing to do with being a loving father", Jeremiah says in a matter-of-fact manner. "He doesn't care about the boy like that. The lad is just a societal symbol to him, something that he can use to manipulate people's impressions of him, another avenue to extract sympathy, respect, or whatever he needs to seal the deal. It's just another reason that returning the young master to his rightful place is more important now, than ever."

Tomes gets up and walks over to a small, dirty window. As he looks out at the noonday sun shining upon the old, abandoned buildings surrounding them, he adds, "As we sit here, Senator Richards is meeting with a trusted few, in the Justice Department, about how this can be used to bring Henry Livingston to answer for his many years of political corruption and fraudulent business dealings. Jim doesn't know how deep the unscrupulous pockets of Livingston are, or how wide his villainous grasp reaches out. But, for years, there have been those who have wanted to bring this graft and deceit to an end. With the buying of a child, the assault and intention to kill a man, and whatever actions that he endorses now, in response to his evil grip on Topeka being shaken, he will be a very dangerous man. I have seen this before when someone has nothing to lose, they purpose to take out as many as they can before they go. As Mr. Jensen so aptly stated, it is imperative that we get you and Seth out of Topeka as fast as we can, and as discreetly as we can."

Rand, suddenly, speaks out, "I know you mean well, but you have to be insane to think that this man, still recovering from some pretty serious injuries, can even attempt to get on a horse and ride away from here. He may never live to see wherever he is headed."

The lawman looks at Barton, who is now leaning on Seth for support, then turns back to the brawny cargo shipper, and replies, "You may be right, he may not live to see Seth back home, again. But, one thing is for sure, he won't live to see anything if Livingston finds him. The raging rich man will finish what was started, that night, up at the mansion. If I know this man, and I think I do pretty well, I think Barton would rather die trying than die doing nothing. Right, cowboy?"

Barton closes his eyes, then puts his arm around Seth, and asks, "It's up to you, son. Do you think you can get us home safely? Or do you think that we should stay and hope for the best?"

Seth, putting down his liniment cloth, stands up, takes Barton by the hand, and answers, "I think it's time to find Smoke and go home, Daddy."

Barton, with a slight smile of pride at observing the grit

being shown by the youngest Anderson, realizes that the horse, in question, has not been accounted for since Barton left him at the Livingston estate.

"Has anyone seen or heard from the big gray one, lately?" Barton poses the question for anyone to answer, as he knows that he doesn't have a clue where Smoke is.

Tomes, holding back an urge to chuckle, remarks that he can't prove it, but he has felt like Smoke may have been following him, and Hickory, for the last day or so. No actual visual sightings, just that sense of being watched by something or someone. And, from time to time, the sound of hooves pounding the Kansas turf like only Smoke might do.

"Again, I wouldn't want to place a large bet on it, but I am feeling pretty confident that, when the time comes and you are ready to leave, Smoke is just one of your high-pitched whistles away from making a sudden appearance, as only he can do."

Barton, getting a supportive look from Seth, says, "Knowing that showoff, I wouldn't be surprised either."

For the next thirty minutes, an undercover plan was developed to get Seth and Barton out of Topeka. As it was going on one o'clock, in the afternoon, Jeremiah figured that Seth would not be missed until around seven, when the family gathered for an evening meal. Henry Livingston never spent any more time with family than he had to, figuring his time was more profitable when he hung out with the other businessmen of Topeka. Mrs. Livingston would be tied up with club card games, luncheonettes, and wine tastings until it was time to gather in the family dining room. This meant that there was between six and seven hours for the missing child to be discovered, the ensuing chaos to be controlled, and a search to be organized. A lot of time for a healthy Barton, on a swift-running Smoke, to put some distance between himself and Topeka.

But that was not the case, this time. Barton could not withstand the full-speed pace of riding Smoke, with his internal injuries still healing. Plus, Smoke would be carrying an injured man, a seven-year-old kid, and the additional provisions that would be needed on a trip that could take two days to complete. So, after a few minutes of discussion, it was decided that a second horse would be needed to transport Seth and carry the extra supplies for the travel. Rand offered one of his best Morgan horses for the journey. While explaining that it would not be a speedy steed, it was a gentle-spirited horse and would carry its special load as far as was needed.

It took another thirty minutes for everyone to be assigned a duty, and then to accomplish it. Rand and Wilbur got the second horse saddled and ready. Jeremiah volunteered to go to a nearby general store and get some foodstuffs that would be appropriate for Barton and Seth. Tomes' chore was to get Barton ready, which included changing bandages, helping with eating one last bowl of Wilbur's concoction, and to discuss a new wrinkle that had been added to the plan to get the Andersons out of the state capital, while drawing as little attention as possible.

Because a mysterious-looking man, a big gray horse, and a child would be too obvious to not draw attention, and just as easy to remember, Rand suggested strapping a small freight box on the Morgan horse, a box just big enough for a small boy to hide in. He would paint the words 'farm tools' on it. While the consensus was it was not the most perfect option, it would offer the most promise, on such short notice.

"Seth, riding in a cargo box tied to a moving horse is not going to be easy. Do you think you can do it?" asked the marshal, as he and the young Anderson helped Barton get dressed for the departure.

"Sure, Marshal Tomes! It is just going to be like when Adam and I play hide-n-seek. I am just going to curl up, be real still, and hope nobody finds me. You think that will be ok?"

Tomes felt a growing lump in his throat, as he heard the young boy talk of something that Seth would never be able to do again. At least, not with his older sibling. The lawman wondered how much this boy knows, and how much will have to be explained to him on the way back to Smithview. Tomes often found himself jealous of Barton, the life that the rancher had once, the close family he was surrounded by. But he did not feel anything but sadness for what his friend would have to do, to prepare his son for the new life that was waiting for them both.

"That's right, you make a game out of it. When you get a few miles out of town, you can let your dad find you. Then you can laugh at him, for not knowing you were there, the whole time."

Tomes looks at Barton, who is standing looking at his boy, probably having the same sobering thoughts that the marshal just had.

As some distant church bell announced the arrival of two o'clock, the small band of co-conspirators gathered to put their contributions upon the awaiting workhorse. Tomes had decided to let Barton just stay in the hiding place and rest until the last possible moment to leave. When all had been loaded and secured, he went back to the simple storage room and informed Barton it was time to leave town, before all hell breaks loose.

As he stepped out into the brilliant sun, for the first time in many days, Barton noticed the three men who had played an important part in his living until this moment. He stepped up to each one, and thanked them for their specific sacrifice for him, and Seth. He turns to summon Smoke, who has not appeared yet, but Barton turns back to the elderly black man, who now has tears welling up in his eyes.

"These two have, probably, sacrificed their business and their livelihood," Barton started, never one for many words. "But you have sacrificed so much more, possibly even your life if Livingston finds you before the law can restrain him. I will not forget that you have given my son back to me. If you ever feel like the ranch life is calling you, Smithview is a good place with good people. You would be welcome there, and you would be protected."

For the first time since Barton had met him, Jeremiah smiled and responded, "I am grateful for your kind suggestion, Mr. Anderson. But I have a need to head home to Mississippi. I understand I have some distant relatives there, from a long limb on the family tree that I did not know of, until recently. Seems they have gotten some available government land and are making a living as tobacco farmers. I am sure I will have to trade in my city attire for country garments, but I can bring some class and dignity to the vocation, don't you think, Mr. Anderson?"

Barton gets that smirk, in the corner of his mouth, touches his finger to the brim of his hat, and turns to summon the only missing piece of the Anderson caravan. With his injured ribs burning as his lungs expand, Barton takes a big breath. He whistles long and high, as he has done many times before.

Nothing.

Worry takes its place on the faces of those watching. All but Barton. He takes another long, deep breath. From his lips comes an even longer, higher call to come to him.

Nothing. Until...

The sound of rapid hooves beating upon the city streets gets louder and louder. Then, around the corner of a distant, collapsed warehouse, races Smoke, whose whinny seems even higher than Barton's call.

Smoke runs up to Barton, places his soft chin in the cowboy's awaiting hand, and then proceeds to do his 'front hoof' dance, showing his pleasure at the sight of his old friend.

"It took you two whistles. You are going to have to work on that," Barton observes, with a false sense of disappointment.

Smoke shakes his head up and down as if to agree with the

statement. Then, the dark horse looks at the smaller Anderson, standing by Barton. The curious equine takes a couple of steps closer, so he can take a few exploratory smells of the temporary stranger. But, when Seth places his arms around Smoke, and gently embraces the horse's face, the comforted steed closes his eyes as if to confidently say...

"I remember you, little one. Where have you been?"

When all of the packing has been done for the long journey, Seth is placed in the cargo box, which has been firmly stationed upon the big Morgan horse. Rand has removed a couple of wooden slats to ensure that the youngster will be able to breathe adequately. Also, a small bag of candy and a canteen of water are placed in the short-term travel apparatus. The young boy gives everyone a salute by putting his hand to his forehead, much like his father does by touching his fingers to the brim of his hat. Everyone, including a slightly grinning Barton, returns the uplifting gesture.

As he helps Barton upon Smoke, Tomes says that he wishes he could join them, but the marshal feels he needs to stay in Topeka. He does not know if Livingston's graft has reached into the U.S. Marshal's office, and Tomes is sure that Senator Richards will need all the help he can get with arresting, and holding, the nefarious businessman. As soon as he felt that the secure apprehension of Livingston had been accomplished, he would try to catch up with Barton, and Seth, as soon as he could.

Barton nodded his understanding, and approval, of the marshal's plan. With one last check that Seth was doing well, Barton waves to those who have helped to make this moment possible pushes his heels into Smoke's sides and proclaims words that he never felt he would ever say.

"Come on, big gray, let's take Seth home to Smithview!"

8

_____

"Daddy, did I do good? Was I quiet so no one would know I was here?"

Barton, with a fake look of surprise at finding his youngest son, replied, "Why, where did you come from? I forgot you were coming along with us."

Seth laughs, and says, "Daddy, you are just having fun with me, aren't you?"

Fun. A word that had not been used in Barton's life for a long time. Nothing about his life, since that morning on the Anderson ranch, has come close to fun. And, while Seth's perspective might see the possibilities of glee in the coming days, Barton could see that this impending adjustment, in his life and Seth's, would be anything but merry. But nothing was going to rob him of this familiar feeling, that was slowly coming back. Barton was a father again, and it felt right to have another Anderson riding next to him.

While they would pass food and water to each other, Barton would not consider making camp until they were at least fifty miles from Topeka, and the sun was almost down. If Jeremiah's guess was right, about the Livingstons not finding out about Seth's absence until seven, then the chaos has begun back in Topeka. Barton figured it was around that time now. He also estimated that he, and Seth, had a few things working in their favor. One, actions born from havoc are never without wasted effort and time. Two, Livingston doesn't know if Seth is still in Topeka, or not. So it could take hours just to discover that fact. Three, if Seth and his abductor have left town, then what direction did they go in? While anyone who is pursuing has a one-in-four chance of getting the direction right, there is a three-in-four chance of getting it wrong, and that means having to backtrack and start over. Of course, Barton knows that 'even a blind hog can get lucky and find an ear of corn', and Livingston could get a lucky roll of the dice, and all of the factors fall in place. But Barton will handle this matter just like he does when he deals with other criminals, just stay calm and patient, for the truth is on his side. When it comes to the rules of this game, Livingston can only guess what his opponent is doing. Barton knows what every move will be in avoiding discovery. And that is the greatest edge that anyone can have.

"I know we have been riding a long time, but do you think you could ride another hour, or so before we make camp and fix us some real food and get a little sleep," Barton asks his young riding companion.

"Yes, sir! I am not tired at all", Seth answers. "And I will be looking for a good place to stop. You know, wood for a fire, water for our canteens. You want me to do that?"

Barton just smiles, and softly responds, "You do that, son."

Meanwhile, back in Topeka, utter hell has broken loose, as Jeremiah had predicted. The rants, of a mad man, ring through the halls of the Livingston mansion. The cries of a woman, unaware of the location of the young master of the estate, are drowned out by the exploding threats and demands of a man who is used to having his every question answered, and his every whim addressed.

"Where is the boy? How in the hell can a seven-year-old kid go missing in a guarded house, with armed morons all around the grounds, and a stone wall lining the perimeter. Where is Jensen? Has anyone seen him? Did he go get the kid from school? Is anyone even paying attention to me? If this is the fault of anyone on my payroll, I will fire every one of them, if I don't have them killed first!"

The ranting, the crying, and the fervent search of the property went on for nearly an hour. Then, one of the house staff comes running up to maniacal Livingston. Clearly, the frantic servant is winded, and physically exhausted, battling to find the ability to report the latest on the search for the missing youngster. Livingston stares at the heaving houseboy, then responds in a way only he is capable of.

"Will you give me a report on the boy, or go somewhere and have a fatal stroke? You are wasting my time!"

"We have searched the entire house, but he is not here", the breathless man begins, "He is not anywhere on the property. We have looked in every room, every corner, every stable, the boy is just not anywhere to be found on the estate grounds."

"That is not good enough, you imbecile! You go look some more and if you can't come back with better news than that, don't come back at all. Is there anyone here that is worth the money I pay you or are you all just wastes of the air your breath?"

Even Mrs. Livingston, who is weeping beyond her control, is not safe from the onslaught of the barbs of the blustering big mouth, who is not even capable of compassion toward his own wife.

"Hannah, will you stop your bawling and make yourself

useful? Sitting there having a breakdown is not going to find the boy. I can't think with you making all that racket. After all, he isn't your kid. If we don't find him, I'll just get you another one!"

As the broken woman runs from the room, wailing even louder, two armed guards enter the room. They walk up to their bellowing boss, who is giving them a look as if to say that 'you better have some good news, or someone is going to start paying dearly'.

"Mr. Livingston, we have talked to all of the staff, the groundskeepers, and the security team, and no one has seen the boy since Jensen took him to school this morning. And it seems no one has seen your head butler since before noon time when he left to run an errand. The boy, nor Jensen, are anywhere to be found. Do you think both of them disappearing could be related?"

Livingston gets up in the face of the reporting guard, who steps back in expectation of a verbal onslaught. "What do you think, genius?" Livingston thunders in the cowering man's face. "Nobody could care less about an old black house servant. Do you think, maybe, that someone may be trying to get at me by taking the boy? Who have I given reason to come against me in such a way?"

"I am sure there are plenty of distinguished candidates to consider, starting with that furniture mover you had roughed up. He seemed to have an interest in the whereabouts of your boy," comes a voice from the back of the dimly lit room.

"Who said that?" Livingston roars. "Who is the fool that dares to interrupt my questioning?"

A lanky, shadowy figure steps out from the guards and Livingston realizes it's the one that is called Hartmann. Livingston remembers hiring him, at the suggestion of one of the other minions who had observed him handling three drunk cowboys who didn't like the way Hartmann was looking at them.

The rich man never enjoyed being around this enigmatic person, but the way he carried his double-holster pistols gave the impression that this was someone who could be of use if the ideal situation called for it.

"Why do you bring up that saddle trash," asked a flustered Livingston. "He was taken care of over a week ago. He is no longer a problem to me!"

"Are you sure?" Hartmann asks, while never changing his dark, dour expression.

Livingston is now confused and retorts, "What are you talking about? Do you know something that I don't know? Why are we talking about a dead cowboy when my boy is missing?"

Livingston discovers that no one in the room wants to answer his question and sees a growing concern appearing on their faces. It took a few seconds, but the realization that a dark secret was being kept from him caused the irate Livingston to lose it.

"Damn it! Are you telling me that I should be worrying about a dead man? Where are Smitty and Jeb, they were supposed to take care of that tall piece of trash. Someone had better get to explaining or you are all fired!"

After a few more moments of nervous silence, one guard steps forward and starts filling in Livingston on the actual status of the supposed disposal of the one called Barton Anderson. Livingston is totally seething when he hears of the possibility of Barton surviving that night and is enraged by the fact that the two unreliable guards have long left Topeka for parts unknown.

"To hell with you, to hell with all of you," huffs Livingston. "Is there anyone here that is worth the money you are paid and can be relied on to do anything right!"

"I can," is the simple reply of Hartmann, as he takes one of his revolvers out and spins the clicking shell cylinder as a show of confidence.

"Please, tell me your master plan or are you just as full of crap as the rest of these morons standing in front of me," a frustrated, and still fuming Livingston probes.

Hartmann calmly walks over to a map of Kansas, hanging on the library wall, and shares a suggestion that if the furniture mover is Barton Anderson and he, somehow, has wound up with the boy, then it would make sense to take the boy back to Smithview. Hartmann figures that if Jackson was taken from school, then Jensen would have to be a part of this, as the head butler was the only one who had the authority to withdraw the kid. At this point, Livingston is listening and starting to feel a plan of action is being hatched.

"So, do you think they are still in Topeka, or have they left the city?" Livingston asks, still enraged but willing to listen to possibilities.

Hartmann taps the map with the barrel of the Colt .45, and responds, "If it were me, I would get out of town as soon as possible. I would count on you getting upset and chasing your tail for a while, buying me more time. But, you see Mr. Livingston, I don't get excited or waste valuable time. He is, probably, not counting on someone being able to stay cool and organize a party to come after him and take the boy away from him, at least this early in the discovery that the boy is missing."

Livingston walks over to where Hartmann is standing, looks at the map, then looks at the calm gunman.

"What will you need, and how long will it take you?"

Hartmann looks over the gathered group of hired guards, looks back at the map of Kansas, and then responds, "I will hand pick four men to go with me, we will need five of the fastest horses you have. We will carry as few supplies as possible, so as to not slow us down. He has, at least, a six-hour advantage on us, but he also has a seven-year-old kid with him. Additionally, after the beating he was given, he hasn't healed from that in just a week. Both will slow him down and may cause him to stop somewhere to rest and eat. If we ride all night, and he is headed in the direction I think he is, then we should catch up with them around noon tomorrow. Considering he will put up a spirited fight for the boy, we should be able to kill him, get the boy, and be back here by this time tomorrow night."

A devilish smile spreads across the face of the rich businessman, and he inquires, "You are pretty sure of yourself, aren't you?"

"I hear he is pretty good with a gun, but so am I," the confident answer comes from the hired gunman. "It will be interesting to see how long Mr. Anderson can hold off his inevitable death."

Livingston, now almost giddy at the prospect of such a happening, proclaims, "This time, tomorrow night, I will be sitting here, with ten thousand dollars waiting for you!"

Hartmann, as he turns to leave the room, nonchalantly utters, "Make it fifteen, and I will give you that big Henry rifle to hang on your trophy wall."

"If you bring me the boy, the rifle, and Jensen's coat soaked in the old black man's blood, I will make it an even twenty thousand! Think you are up to that, gunslinger?" Livingston asks, in almost a challenging tone.

As he exits the library, Hartmann never turns or answers, he just throws his right hand up in a salutation of goodbye.

As plans start coming together in Topeka, Barton and Seth are making camp for the night. Although every effort has been made to travel as far away as possible, the significant injuries that Barton sustained, at the hands of Livingston's men, are still limiting them from covering as much trail as Barton wishes they could. He is not remotely confident that they have traveled to the point that they are beyond the prospects of an eventual confrontation. Barton remembers how he felt, when his family was taken from him, and how he was committed to finding those who did it. He was prepared to travel the globe if that is what it took. The one thing that separates Barton from Livingston may be the one thing that decides how this ordeal meets its conclusion. Livingston is operating from a severely bruised ego, and he wants personal revenge. Barton, on the other hand, was motivated by his family getting justice, which could only be realized through vindication. He knows that the first man who makes a mistake, in this encounter, will be the one who goes home empty-handed, if they go home at all.

"You just take it easy, daddy. I am going to take care of the horses, gather some kindling wood, and get a fire started for supper. While the beans cook, I will run to that nearby stream and get some fresh water. If you think the beans are done, while I am gone, do you think you can take the pan off of the fire? I don't know about you, but I am hungry enough to eat those beans cold, but the bacon might be a little too raw, ha-ha"

"It will be just fine, son," was Barton's pleased reply as he watched his remaining offspring exhibit such acts of maturity. Barton has wondered if it would be difficult for Seth to adjust to living away from the life of house staff, tutors, five-course meals, and recitals. But this seven-year-old has proven what Barton has said, all along, "Seth is an Anderson, he always has been, and his bloodline will raise him above any situation that he is put in."

After a hearty meal was enjoyed, Seth washed the dishes and laid them by the campfire to dry. Then, he checked on his healing father to make sure there weren't any medical needs to be taken care of. Barton assured Seth that he was doing well, under the circumstances, but that he would let his young medic take a look at him before they loaded up and left in the morning. One more log was placed on the fire before Seth sat down on his bedroll, which was conveniently placed next to Barton's, just in case something needed attending to before the sun came up.

Barton looked at Seth, who was gazing into the crackling fire, reminiscent of what his father does when there are things to contemplate and unknowns to be considered. The youngest Anderson even sits with his legs positioned just like Barton, with his arms lying across his knees. Because he was the older sibling, Adam was the one who went with Barton to gather the livestock, fix a fence, or hunt for wild game to smoke, jerk, or cold-pack away in the underground cellar. Jenny had often said she could see more of Barton in Seth, than she could in Adam. Barton never gave it much thought, as the boys were equal in his eyes, never favoring one over the other. It was just that Adam was capable of doing more things around the ranch. But, after watching Seth make camp, take care of the horses, and cook their meals, Barton realizes that Seth's time to take part in everyday life may be here, whether either of them was ready or not.

"You sleepy?" Barton asked, wondering if this was the suitable time to engage his son in inquisitorial conversation So many things that Barton feels he should know, so he can try to understand how to approach the future, from a paternal perspective. For a long time, Barton had only had to consider the thoughts, concerns and. opinions of one person, himself. Now, natural impulse and intuition will have to be replaced by a new regard for making decisions-how will they affect Seth?

"No, Daddy, I'm not sleepy, not one bit," Seth replied as he turned on his bedroll and faced Barton. "Are you hurting? Do I need to change any old bandages? Maybe you'd like some water? Just tell me and I will go get it faster than a flyswatter gets a June bug!"

Repressed emotions rise up in Barton's mind and heart when he grasps what Seth said. The 'June bug' expression was something that Jenny always said, a catchphrase to let someone know she wasn't too busy to help. Maybe, just maybe, Seth hasn't been away from 'the Anderson life' so long that the young boy, sitting in front of him, has forgotten what was, and could be again.

"No, son, I am fine," Barton answered. "Just wondered if you were alright. I know today has been filled with a lot of surprises and changes. Are you good with things, as far as leaving Topeka? That was a pretty impressive life you had back there. I would imagine you had, pretty much, anything a growing boy could ever want, and then some. Right?"

Seth made a slight frown upon hearing his father's question. His retort came swiftly.

"Not really, sir. I couldn't do anything without someone's permission or someone having to be there, watching every move I made. I never got to go riding, except within some big walls that surrounded the place. And, when I did ride, I had to ride a pintsize pony that was meant for little kids. Can you believe that? It was kind of embarrassing. I never went fishing, frog gigging, catching fireflies, or played games with other kids. I, basically, went to school, went to dinner when the bell rang, and went to bed. I wouldn't say that was very impressive, would you?'

Barton bit his lower lip, to keep from chuckling out loud, especially at Seth's implicit statement about ponies being for 'little kids'. Barton repositioned himself, where he could lean more on his saddle, in case this opportunity to converse lasted for any length of time.

"Was there ever a time that you considered running away?" Barton carefully inquired. "Maybe tell someone that you were from Smithview, and you wanted to go back home?"

Seth shook his head, in a negative expression, and looked at his father with a countenance that told Barton that what was coming next would be daunting to hear.

"No sir, until I saw you today, going home never seemed possible. When I met him, Mr. Livingston told me that I didn't have a family anymore. He said that drunken, savage Indians came to the ranch, while you were gone with a posse. He told me that they had killed other families that day and that I was lucky that I was found by some riders that were after the renegades. I was informed that I should be glad that I had a chance at a better life, and I was not allowed to ever talk about the past again."

Barton is captivated by Seth's resolve as the young boy remembers the facts of the past year. As he listens, Barton is brought to mind of Jenny, as she had that innate ability to address a situation with clarity and purpose. Although Jenny could be strong and concise to those who needed her strength, he had found that she could slip away to have her moments of tender commiseration. But, once she had regained her composure, she would return to offer her continued advocacy. Barton will keep this in mind as he considers how far to let this venture of fact-finding go with Seth.

Barton, knowing what Livingston has told his son is nothing but self-serving hogwash, will continue forward with that spurious version, so as not to throw Seth into a state of confusion or worse.

"Do you recall much about the morning that you were taken from the ranch?" Barton asks, trying to tread carefully as he pushes the conversation forward.

"All I remember is that Adam and I were asleep upstairs, then Mom was yelling for us to go out the attic window, climb down from the roof, and run to the barn. Once we got to the barn, there was a lot of yelling and shooting outside. Adam put his hands over my ears, for a minute. Then, he told me to run to the underground cellar and stay there until I heard from him. I was scared, but I ran as fast as I could, got into the cellar, and hid behind the potato box. I stayed there for a long time."

Barton is listening, intently, and finding it harder to breathe as Seth continues with his narration of that morning's events.

"I stayed hidden, in the cellar, waiting for Adam to come get me. When he didn't, and there hadn't been any shooting or yelling for a while, I crawled out from behind the potato box, opened the cellar door, and went outside. I started walking toward the house, but these three men came riding up, one with a red bandana reached down and hauled me up on his horse, and another loud one told me I was going with them, and don't be any trouble. Daddy, I never did see any Indians, just those rather nasty-smelling, foul-mouthed riders. And I don't think they were as nice as Mr. Livingston wanted me to think. That night, they got really drunk, and started talking about things that scared me, bad things that I knew good people didn't do. They said some things about Momma, Adam, and Pawpaw, but I couldn't understand their boozed-up mumbling and laughing. So, when they were asleep, I gathered what things I could and slipped out of camp. I remembered what you taught me, and Adam, about 'keep your eyes on the North star and the Big Dipper" and 'follow running water downstream'. I think I could have made it, if it hadn't been for that dog-gone snake. Of all the things to step on! If I had Adam's gun, I would have blasted it!"

Barton smiled at Seth's opinion of the unplanned rattler, but he knew there were still some somber places that would have to be navigated in this quest for truth and order.

"Didn't you know that I would come after you, no matter where you were or how long it took," Barton asks, trying not to cast any doubt upon Seth or his actions.

"Sir, they told me you were dead, too. Mr. Livingston told me, soon after we got to the big house, that you had been killed by the outlaws that you had gone after. It wasn't until, earlier today, that Marshall Tomes told me that you had come to get me, had been hurt, and that he was going to take me to you. Oh, there were times I dreamed that you, and Smoke, would come riding up. But I really didn't expect that was going to happen. I'm sorry for not believing good enough, Daddy."

Barton, swallowing hard to get that growing lump out of his throat, reached over, took Seth's hand, and replied, "Son, you didn't know. But, I am here now, and that's all that matters."

Suddenly, Seth tilts his head, looks up at Barton, and asks, "Daddy, if they lied about you being dead, then does that mean that they lied about Momma, Adam, and Pawpaw? Are they at the ranch waiting for us to come home?"

Suddenly, Barton's composure is wavering, causing him to look away from his inquisitive son. After taking a moment to pull himself together, Barton turns to his awaiting son and, reluctantly, answers.

"No, Son, they weren't lying about that part. Your momma, Adam, and Pawpaw are not at the ranch. They aren't with us anymore."

With that dispiriting revelation, Seth's shoulders slump, his head falls forward and he sits in silence. After a couple of moments, he lifts his head and asks, "Do you think it would be ok to go to sleep now? I don't feel like talking anymore."

Barton replies, "That would be fine. You get some sleep. We will talk again tomorrow when you feel more like it."

As the growing frustration sinks in, Barton watches as Seth lays down and pulls his blanket over his small body. After getting comfortable, there is no movement, no talking, no sounds of any kind until...

"Daddy, do you think Momma, Adam, and Pawpaw are in Heaven, now?"

"Yes, Seth. They are in Heaven, and you will see them again, someday."

Again, there was silence in the cool Kansas night, nothing but the crackling of the burning campfire. Then, a sound rips through the tranquil darkness, and tears through Barton's heart, taking the very breath from the tall man.

Seth, softly, crying.

As his heart aches for his child, Barton curses an evil dead outlaw, who from the grave, seems to still be able to hurt his family.

"Burn in hell, Angus Ford. Burn in hell, you son-of-a-bitch!"

9

———

The Kansas sun is rising above the horizon when the Andersons start stirring around the campsite. While he knew that every minute that he could put between himself and Topeka was critical, Barton understood that he was traveling with a seven-year-old and not a seasoned trail rider. Casting aside any physical needs or challenges that the tall man might have, Barton was becoming more adept at putting Seth at the forefront of any, and all, considerations for this trip.

Barton has observed that Seth has been noticeably quiet since being awakened, outside of an occasional 'Yes, sir' or 'No, sir'. Any prolonged discussions between the two will be initiated by the younger traveler, or at least that was Barton's original thought. But, about an hour after resuming their journey, Barton noticed an uneasy look on his son's face. When his concern bests his patience, Barton prompts Smoke to walk up beside Seth and decides to see if it is time to open up a dialogue with the junior Anderson.

"What is on your mind, son?"

Seth didn't respond immediately. It was a couple of minutes before a heart-rending answer came.

"Daddy, if you weren't dead, like they told me, why didn't you come and get me sooner?"

Whether Seth had dwelt on this hypothesis overnight, or it just came to him this morning, Barton knows that this interpretation of uncertain events cannot be allowed to linger in the young boy's mind. Seth's mental resolve has had to process so much, in such a short amount of time. Somewhere, inside his son, Barton knows is a solid foundation that he, and Jenny, spent a lot of time, and love, building. The last year has dealt many blows to Seth's perception of what real life is all about. One of the foundational blocks that Barton will now test is honesty, which had always been a priority between Barton, Jenny, and the boys.

Barton takes a slow, deep breath. Then, he starts a story that he has not looked forward to telling, but he knows that this is a bridge that has to be crossed. If not, then he and Seth will never have any kind of trusting relationship. The divide will be too wide to cross as they start a new, and challenging way of life together.

"Son, I know you are young, very young. And all I can hope for is that if not today, if not tomorrow, someday you will understand what has happened in the last year. It has not been easy. I have not been the best man that I could have been. And because of that, I am afraid that the road has been filled with many surprises, snares, and mis-steps. All I ask is for you to listen to what I have to say, consider each detail on its merit, and judge me on being the man you once knew, not necessarily what I am today."

As Smoke and the Morgan horse walk in rhythm with each other, Barton tells of how he returned to the Anderson ranch that morning. Without going into all of the heart-wrenching details, he shares how the sight of his entire family killed, or taken, was a sorrow that overwhelmed everything that was good in him. Barton explained that the grief of losing everyone he loved broke him, almost killing him from the inside out. As Seth listened intently, his dad tells of how rage, and an intense hunger for revenge, filled the void that was in his heart. All that mattered was finding who had done this terrible thing to his family, and making them pay for it. Filled with hate and feeling he had nothing to lose anymore, Barton told of riding Smoke for weeks, looking for the men who had been to the ranch. Then the three men were located, vengeance was dealt, three men were killed, and Barton was seriously wounded in the process. By this time, Seth's eyes were as big as silver dollars, and he hadn't said a word until Barton refrained from his storytelling to let his young companion understand what he had been told, so far.

After they had ridden a couple of miles, the entire time having no words traded between them, Seth finally broke the silence.

"But, when you found the men who hurt Mommy, Adam, and Pawpaw, didn't you wonder where I was? When you got better from being hurt, didn't you even think about looking for me?"

Feeling the sense of swelling disappointment and confusion in Seth's voice, Barton replied, "Well, son, you and I have had our fair share of heartless liars putting their two cents into what was going on. Where you were misled by Livingston and those men who took you from the ranch, I was told that you had died from your snake bite. I hope you know that I would have come for you, had I known. As a matter of fact, the moment I found out the truth, I jumped on Smoke and have spent the last two weeks looking for you. And, due to the right people and circumstances falling into the right places, here you and I are together. I hope you will understand some of what has gone on in the last year."

Seth is quiet for a minute, as the two continue to ride toward Smithview. Then, the young lad's face takes on a look of realization, as if a load had been lifted from his innocent shoulders.

"Boy, Daddy, things can really get messed up when people just want to pull your leg when they talk to you, can't they?"

Barton smiles at Seth's honest appraisal of what has kept them apart for so long, and his gracious attitude toward those who have played a cruel part in their separation.

"Yep, it sure can get messed up, but you and I will always tell the truth as long as we are together."

It would be a couple of hours later when Barton would, carefully, attempt to impart the remaining truths that needed to be addressed. After taking a break to stretch their legs, check saddle straps and cinches, and munch on some corncakes that Wilbur had packed in Topeka, the two travelers mounted up and resumed their journey. Up to this point, nothing more than idle chatter had been offered. Barton, remembering how well their discussion had gone earlier that morning, decides to engage his young son in another personal exercise of preparing Seth for what life will be like when they get to the ranch in Smithview.

"Seth, I am really proud of how you have handled everything that has been put on you. From being taken from the ranch, having strange people take you into their different way of living, to us being together now. You have been quite the young man, and I just wanted to say that. I wish I could tell you that all the continual adjusting is over, but I need to talk to you about something else that will have to take some getting used to. You up to it?"

Seth looks at Barton, with a cautious trust, and asks, "Will what you tell me make me sad?"

"I don't know," comes the honest, searching response." I

think you might be disappointed, maybe even unhappy. But I don't think it is something that will hurt your heart, like some of the things that we have talked about before. I am hoping it is something that will just take some adjusting to make it work. But, I think, between the two of us, we can do it."

Seth, flashing the Anderson smirk that his father is known for, innocently declares, "Seeing that I have grown up a lot, since the last time you saw me, I am willing to do my part from here on out!"

Barton just shakes his head, in continual amazement at how Seth has handled it all, so far. The reality sinks in that, due to events that he wouldn't wish upon any child, Seth may have had to make the jump from 'kid to a young man' without the chance of just 'being a boy'. Somewhere in the back of his mind, Barton hopes that there will be times when his namesake will be able to enjoy the things of adolescence, and not have to always be recovering from the deeds of heartless adults.

For the next hour, Barton explained about how things would have to be when they get to Smithview. As his dad told of the Curt Sanders situation, the trial, the deal to get out of prison, and the dangers of what Barton does for the state, Seth vacillated between confused, upset, and accepting.

"So, I won't ever get to do things with you, like hunting, fishing, feeding the calves?" Seth asked, rather apprehensively.

Barton, understanding that this is a lot to spring on his young son and that Seth is trying to cling to some dreams he has always had but is seeing most of them go by the wayside, replies.

"I am not going to say we will never get to do some of those things. It's just that we will have to be careful when, and where, we do them. While most people can accept what I have to do, to stay out of prison, there are some who can't and some who don't want me to do it. And those people, mainly the outlaws that I go after, are willing to do what they can to keep me from being successful. That includes having me put back in prison, maybe shooting me, or even hurting those close to me. I just got you back, son. You are all I have, and I will do whatever I have to do to keep you safe. I hope we can dwell on the times we are together more than the times we are apart."

"Does this mean that I won't be living on the ranch, because you have to be gone and I would be there by myself?" Seth quizzes, still trying to put this ever-growing puzzle together, longing to see the complete picture of his future.

"Actually, you will be going home to live on the ranch. Jeff and Sally are running it now. Your Pawpaw gave it to your mother and me, and it just seemed right that they should take their place there, keep it in the family. They are looking forward to having you live with them, growing up with your cousins, Michael and Steven. I bet you will get to do a lot of hunting, fishing, and ranch things with Jeff and the boys. Doesn't that sound like something better than what you left in Topeka?"

Seth contemplates this new information, rolling it around in his budding mind, then answers, "Yes, Sir. Jeff and Sally were always good to us when Adam and I would visit them with Momma. And Michael and Steven love to do a lot of the things that we liked to do. So, it sounds like it will be like home, except..."

Seth's voice, gradually, trails off as he remembers those who won't be there, waiting.

"I know, it is never going to be the same as it was before. But that doesn't mean that it won't be a fine place to hang your hat. They have your bed ready for you, Jeff says he has an eye on a spring buckskin that would make a good horse for you, once he breaks it for riding. Sally has always been a pretty good cook, a better-than-average horseshoe player, and, most importantly, they are family. Like everything else, it's going to take some adjusting to, but it could wind up being more favorable than we could even imagine. I say we give it a try, what do you say?"

Seth's lips tighten and his head tilts slightly, as a vexing truth manifests itself in his mind and his weary heart.

"But, you are not going to be there, are you? Will you not ever come and visit us there, again?"

Barton realizes that this will, probably, be the detail that will always be the 'fly in the ointment'. While it would be more home-like if Barton lived there, it would be a perilous place if he lived there, always wondering if the next riders were there to look at horses, or there to take Barton's life or one of those who lived there.

"No, son. If all goes as planned, I will never set foot on the ranch again. I will keep my distance so people will think that I have abandoned you, the ranch, and the memories that were made there. There is no other way that will offer the best odds of keeping you safe, trust me."

Seth, for a few moments, shakes his head from side to side, trying to take in what sounds like something that is non-negotiable. At least, for now, the youngest Anderson accepts this concept, so he can move on to his next topic of concern.

"If you are not going to live on the ranch, where will you live? How will we ever see each other? How will I know where to go if you want to see me?"

Barton senses that frustration is building up in Seth, that they may have 'bitten off more than the young boy can chew', with what has been shared up to this point. After taking a break to let them both breathe and regroup, Barton attempts to address this latest query.

"Right now, I don't live anywhere in particular. But, when I come to that area to meet Marshal Tomes, I have made me a place up at Rooster Pass. Do you remember the cave we found when we were up there hunting white-tail deer to dress for winter? Well, it makes a great shelter to stay out of sight. There is a running spring inside, it's cool in the summer and naturally ventilates, so I can keep a fire in the winter. Now, it will make a satisfactory place to meet up."

It is plain to see that the wheels in Seth's mind are turning as the young boy's eyes are darting back and forth as if he would see the answer to his next questions if he looked hard enough. Barton has no idea what the young Anderson may be thinking, or considering. He just prepares himself for the next round of honest quizzing.

"Daddy, Rooster Pass is a long way from the ranch house. How will I know you are there? How will I know how to find you, if you want to see me?"

Finally, Barton gets the feeling that Seth is becoming more understanding of their situation, and is more willing to participate in this strategy that is being presented to him. Barton's instincts are telling him that the next part of the plan will, easily, gain his son's approval.

"Well, we are going to need some help, from an old friend, to pull this off. Do you remember when I would go work on the ranch, by myself, and would realize that I needed some help to get the work done? What did I do?"

Seth thought for a second, and then excitedly answered, "You sent Smoke to the house to get Adam! Are you going to send Smoke to get me?"

Barton, enjoying seeing his boy revel in a buoyant moment, decides to have some fun and milk it for what he can. Up to this point, during their journey, not much can be mistaken for being merriment. The change in Seth's countenance tells Barton that this is a welcome opportunity to embrace some hope that the future is looking brighter.

"Well, I don't know, Seth. Smoke doesn't do anything that he doesn't want to do. I have to ask him, really nice, if I need him to do anything for me. Do you think you can ask him to come and get you, and bring you to our meeting place?"

Pulling over on the reins of the Morgan horse that he is riding, Seth leans over as far as he can. Looking back at his father for one last head nod of encouragement, Seth grins and makes his earnest appeal to the big gray stallion.

"Smoke, do you think, if Daddy wants me to come to the cave to visit him, that you could come to the ranch, pick me up, and take me to him? I would really appreciate it and would give you one of your favorite carrots, fresh from the cellar, if you would. What do you say, Smoke?"

Smoke, right on cue, whinnied and threw his head up and down, as if to say that he could be counted on to do his part in this great reunion plan.

Seth laughed out loud, and Barton gave in to a broad smile. Smoke continued to whinny and bob his head up and down, as they continued to ride toward their goal of a new life in Smithview. Even the Morgan horse seemed to sense an upturn in the mood of this band of travelers.

It was just after the noon hour, the sun was straight up in the sky when Barton first noticed it. His initial thought was it was just some area hunters, off in the distance, as he detected the sound of guns being fired. Then, another sound caused him to come to a different chilling realization.

Zing...Zing...

Without any hesitation, Barton guides Smoke over next to the Morgan horse, reaches over with one hand, pulls Seth off, and positions him in front of him. Once his son is firmly in place, the tall man starts laying his heels into the sides of the big gray horse, and yells...

"Run fast, Smoke, run fast!"

Within seconds, Smoke's mighty legs are moving so fast that it seemed as if his feet were barely touching the Kansas terrain.

His powerful muscles were rippling, underneath his skin, as he carried his two riders as swiftly as he possibly could.

"Daddy, what's wrong? Why are we running so fast?

Barton didn't have the time to explain, nor did he have the desire to clarify that he had been mistaken about hearing the gunfire of hunters. One shot in their direction would be a case of bad luck or bad aim. As he continues to hear repeated bullets flying past them, Barton is convinced that they are being, purposefully, fired upon.

Zing...Zing...Zing

"Daddy, should I be afraid? Should I pray?"

"Just hang on tight, son! And, yes to both of your questions!"

Barton doesn't know who is targeting them, but he is pretty sure who has sent them. The one thing that he does know is that Smoke is one of the fastest animals around, but even the big gray can't outrun a pursuing bullet. Searching frantically, Barton sees the remains of an old stone field fence, in the distance. If they can make it, that could offer some kind of cover until he can think of a proper response to this abrupt assault. But another collection of sounds will be the foreshadowing of some of the direst moments in this traveling duo's future.

Bang...Zing...Thump

Instantly, Smoke lets out a pained, high-pitched squeal, a sound that Barton has never heard his equine companion make. The big horse's running rhythm is disrupted, quickly becoming a disjointed combination of a trot and a limp. Knowing that they don't have a chance without cover, Barton takes the only action that he can. Grabbing the lengthy reins in one hand, he starts laying the toughened leather into his faithful, but failing friend. First, one side and then the other.

"Don't go down, Smoke! You can't go down!"

"Daddy, why are you whipping Smoke? What did he do?"

Just as they make it behind the aged limestone fence,

Smoke's mighty legs collapse underneath him, sending Barton and Seth tumbling across the ground. Seth is thrown clear, temporarily having the breath knocked out of him. Barton, unfortunately, is not as lucky. His trajectory is abruptly halted when he slams up against the rock field wall. Barton groans as he rebounds off the unforgiving stone structure. Pain swells up inside him, and soon blood is trickling out of the side of his mouth. He quickly wipes his mouth before Seth can see it.

While Barton and Seth try to regain their senses, the bullets continue to fly over their heads. Occasionally, limestone dust and sparks will fly in the air, as their stalkers lower their aim toward the targets behind the field fence.

Bang...Bang...Bang...Bang!

"Are you all right, son?" Barton asks as he crawls across the ground toward the wounded Smoke. The great horse is now lying on his side, gasping for breath and making no attempt to get up.

"Other than some scratches, I think I am ok. How is Smoke doing? What is going on, Daddy?"

Trying to stay as low as he can, out of the line of fire of the unknown predators, Barton reaches out and pulls his Henry rifle from its sheath. Once he has the long gun in his control, he reaches over and opens his saddle bag, removing two boxes of .44 caliber shells. It was then that Barton noticed the blood oozing out of Smoke, right behind his right shoulder. While he has a great concern for the fallen stallion, Barton's priority is Seth and figuring out how to overcome the onslaught of gunfire that continues to rain down on them.

Bang...Bang...Bang...Bang...Bang!

Barton pulls himself back to the stone barrier, where Seth is waiting for any encouraging words that his dad might be able to offer. When he sees the fear and uncertainty in the youngster's eyes, Barton hands Seth his hat and says, "Hold that for me, while I see how much trouble those curs are in for messing with a couple of Andersons on our way home."

Seth's look of concern melts into a slight smile that says he is glad he is with his dad, again.

"I want you to stay hunkered down and out of sight. I think we can hold them off, for now. There is a lot of open space between us and them, and those few trees don't give them very good coverage. If you remember what I taught you about loading guns, especially the Henry, then I will do the shooting and you can keep me supplied with the ammo. You think you can do your part?"

"Yes sir, but who is going to take care of Smoke?" Seth asks, as he glances at the big gray horse, still laying on its side and making stressed neighing sounds

"There is nothing we can do for him, right now," Barton replies, trying to console the youngster while hiding his own. angst about the state of his riding partner. "They want me to get up and try to help him, they would love for me to do that and give them a clear shot. But, the best chance Smoke has is for you and me to stay strong, stay smart, and do enough damage to them to cause them to give up, or give out."

And, with that thought and resolve, a long afternoon begins.

10

———

"Hey rancher, give us the boy and I promise to put you, and your big horsey, out of your misery, nice and quick!"

"Hey bounty hunter, that rifle is going to look good over Mr. Livingston's fireplace!"

"Hey vigilante, give me the damn kid or I will tie you, and that buzzard-bait horse, out where they can pick your eyes out!"

Such were the taunts and goads that the hired gunman hurled at Barton, hoping to rattle him or cause him to make a mistake that could be taken advantage of. But, waiting and determination are two character traits that Barton has refined over the last year, or so. Usually, when an opponent starts yapping and speaking insults, that is a sign that there is a hidden doubt somewhere in that man's mind. Barton will let his unknown assailant continue to talk about his unavailing intimidation. When the time is right, as many times before, Barton will let the Henry rifle speak for him.

The cyclical gunfire, from Livingston's henchmen, continues

for another half-hour. While the noise was intimidating, the result was that they weren't getting any closer to hitting their target. But Barton did notice that the longer their impotent attack went on, the younger Anderson's bravery was showing signs of wearing down, under the constant onslaught.

"Cover your ears, son. It's time to let them know we are still here," as Barton turns, lifts the long gun over the stone wall, and commences to reply the only way he knows how.

Ka-boom...Ka-boom...Ka-boom...Ka-boom!

"I'm hit, Hartmann. I'm hit, bad, "came the cries of one of the cohorts of the hired gunman.

"Shut up, you halfwit," Hartmann snarls, frustration starting to swell up in him! "Get back up against that tree and start shooting back!"

"I can't! I am gut-shot, and I am bleeding bad. I ain't no good like this, I need a doctor. We have got to give up on the boy and get me to a doctor!"

Bang...Bang!

"Now, you don't need a doctor, you just need an undertaker," the cold-hearted gunman said. The other Livingston riders look on in shock, as their friend lay dead.

"Hey rancher, we put our wounded out of their misery! Just like you are going to have to do for that plug horse, very soon!"

Barton looks over at Seth, who is worried, but trying to stay strong for his father. A glance at Smoke tells him that, although Hartmann is trying to be cruel and unsettling, there is some truth in what the hardened gunman said. All of their supplies are on the Morgan horse, and there is no telling where it is at the moment, especially with all the yelling and gunfire that has been transpiring. The few medical supplies, that were packed for Barton's care, might have been helpful in trying to give Smoke a chance to live.

"Daddy, did that man shoot one of his own people?" Seth asked?

"Yes, son. If I am guessing right, there are now four out there. If they lose one more, I am hoping the other two will give up on the loudmouth, and leave. They called him Hartman. Does his name or voice sound familiar to you?"

Seth shook his head, in the affirmative, and replied, "I think it's the shady one who wears two guns and doesn't say too much. I don't think anyone cared for him, but they seemed to be afraid of him. He was kind of like the class bully at school. You stay away from the bully, don't rile him if you do run into him, and let everyone else think that he is partial to you."

Barton half-smiled at Seth's analyses of their current nemesis. Figuring that the three co-riders, with Hartmann, are either scared, mad, or confused over what happened to their friend, Barton lifts the Henry rifle over the stone wall and commences to continue his previous .44 caliber conversation.

Ka-boom...Ka-boom...Ka-boom...Ka-boom!

Barton listens for sounds that might give an indication that his latest volley of shots has found their marks. Within a few moments, confirmation is established on one result, along with a sense of a growing mutiny among his attackers.

"Hey, Hartmann, you cold-hearted bastard! Lewis just took one in the throat. You aren't going to have to worry about putting him out of his misery like you did Emory.

"It's time to quit messing around," the professional gunslinger barks! "I will pin him down, with gunfire, while you and Homer rush him. Once you get beyond the stone fence, I will follow you, kill the vigilante, get the kid, and ride out of here!"

"Here is a better idea," replied the one called Jonesy. "You rush him while he is filling the air with that Henry rifle. Homer and I have decided it's time to ride back to Topeka and get more men and guns. I don't think this is going quite as smoothly as you thought it would, gunman!"

Hartmann, seeing his chance at the twenty thousand dollar reward disintegrating, growls, "He is only one damn man, only one gun. He is, probably, busted up again, his horse is near dead, their supplies are gone, and he has a seven-year-old to worry about. He has absolutely nothing going in his favor, you coward!"

"For a man who has nothing going for him, he seems to be doing pretty dang good," remarked Jonesy. "Especially, compared to what we have gotten accomplished. We shot his horse, and he has played a part in the death of forty percent of your hand-picked militia. The rancher isn't going anywhere, as you said. Let's go back, let Livingston yell all he wants. We will regroup, and return with more firepower. This time, tomorrow night, we will have the boy and the reward."

Hartmann, slowly, appraises the status of the situation, not wanting to go as far as conceding he has underestimated the adversary on the other side of the rock barrier. After a few moments of reluctant reflection, the hardened gunman decides to launch one more taunt toward Barton.

"You are in a hell of a mess, bounty hunter! That kid is going to have to watch you, and that sorry horse, die right in front of him. His last memory of you is going to be how inept you were, how you were a failure as a father to him. When we come back, he will be crying and begging for us to take him away from his dead daddy. Chew on that, big man!"

Ka-boom…Ka-boom…Ka-boom!

"Hey Hartmann, you pompous ass," Jonesy calls out! "I hope Homer enjoyed your hot-air blustering because that is the last thing he got to hear before the rancher put a rifle slug through his ear! If you are done pissing off the man with the Henry, can we go before there is no one left to go back!"

Once they secure the three bodies, of their dead comrades, to their horses, Hartmann and Jonesy mount up and take off. Barton will wait until the sound of galloping horses is out of earshot before he will get up to check on Seth and Smoke. He steps toward the young boy, who looks like he has been through a haunted cornfield, but Seth waves his hand, signaling that he is alright and for his dad to check on Smoke.

As he knelt by the wounded horse, Barton sensed that his riding companion was in a dire state. Rubbing Smoke's trembling chin, it was easy for Barton to assess that the big gray was struggling to breathe, as there was a foam starting to form around his mouth. When he inserted his finger into the horse's nostril, he discovered droplets of blood when he withdrew it. With just those few indicators, Barton suspects that Smoke has taken a bullet to the lung. As there is no chance that it passed through the horse's massive body, not only is there concern for the damage, but also for lead dissolving into his system.

"Daddy, is Smoke going to die?"

Barton finds himself being beset with so many feelings, both new and old dormant ones. He has never considered being without Smoke. He, always, figured that he would be the one to bow out of the duo, especially since taking on the 'janitor' role. In the seven years since the gangly colt came into the world, this moment has never been a consideration. And, even though the events of the last year have made Barton's heart colder and harder, he realizes that he will always have a special place for his travel partner, as Smoke lays helpless before him.

"I don't know, son. I just don't know. We have until tomorrow until Livingston's riders come back. I have got to try to find the Morgan horse, as that is our only supply and way to ride out of here. You think you will be alright while I am gone?"

Seth, taking a big breath, responds, "Yes, sir! I will gather firewood and make a campsite. I will go see if there is any water nearby, as I am sure we will need some for Smoke and us."

Barton, looking at the struggling horse lying upon the ground, remarks, "I will help with the campsite when I get back. In the meantime, would you mind sitting with Smoke? Just hold his head in your lap, and talk calmly to him. I think if he hears you and feels you nearby, it will be a comfort to him."

Seth, sitting slowly down by Smoke's head and pulling it onto his lap, answers, "Sure, Dad! Me and Smoke will be right here when you get back. We will be just fine."

Barton turns to leave, in search of the Morgan horse. Abruptly, Barton turns back toward Seth, sitting on the ground. Pulling his Colt out of its holster, he cocks it and hands it to the surprised youngster.

"It is loaded, and it is ready. Keep it near you. If you, or Smoke, have any problems or emergencies, fire it in the air and I will come back as fast as I can. If any strangers, and I mean anyone you have never seen before, come riding up in a way that concerns you, then you put a bullet in them. Don't threaten them, don't wave it at them, but put a .45 slug in them. We will work out the details later. Do you understand?'

"Yes, sir! No threats, no questions, just shoot and wait for you, right?"

Barton smirks, and says, "Yes, son. I'll be back soon."

Seth watched as his father walked out of sight, his youthful mind wary of the situation that they found themselves in. Although Barton had tried to be discreet about it, Seth had seen his dad wiping fresh blood from his mouth. Could Barton have bitten his lip when they fell off of Smoke? Yeah, that had to be it, because Adam bit his lip, once, when they were chasing each other, and the older Anderson son tripped and fell. Once the medicine kit is found, Seth concludes that a lot of things will be better for it, including the hurting horse with its head in the boy's lap.

"You have got to get better, Smoke," Seth implored as he ran his hand between the horse's ears. "I have never gotten to ride you, by myself. Adam got to ride you, remember that? You would come to the house when Daddy needed help. I was so jealous, but when I would say anything, Daddy would say that my day would come. When we get home, I promise I am going to give you a good bath, brush you, give you your favorite feed with those little bits of molasses in it. Doesn't that sound good, boy? I love you Smoke, please don't die."

Smoke tries to lift his head, in an effort to give the concerned youngster a sign of encouragement. But all he can manage is a noise that can, at best, be described as a cross between a weak whinny and a deep cough. The Kansas sun would slowly set upon this image of a small boy embracing this dynamic equine creature.

It would be, almost, ninety minutes before Barton finds the Morgan horse, grazing by a thicket of Chokeberry bushes. Once he observes that all of the supplies are still secure upon the brawny horse, Barton eases upon the saddle. Although the pain inside him is excruciating, he knows he has to get back to Seth, and Smoke, as quickly as possible. As when they were riding before, Barton prompts his ride into an easy gallop, so as not to cause him any additional pain or injury. Another thirty minutes will pass before Barton returns to the stone field fence, where he finds Seth still holding Smoke's head in his lap and trying to comfort the big gray stallion.

"How are you doing, son?"

Seth, with a deep look of concern on his young face, answers, "I am doing alright. I have been rubbing Smoke and talking to him. I tried singing a few Sunday School songs, but he just lays here. He isn't shaking or making that gasping noise anymore, is that a good sign?"

Barton doesn't answer his son's inquiry, for he knows that Smoke has slipped into what Dr. Tilley would refer to as 'a state of shock'. Between the loss of blood and any internal damage, a body will go into a state of self-protection, seemingly shutting down any parts that are not essential to survival. Barton is convinced that that is what has happened to Smoke.

Barton gets off of the Morgan horse and kneels beside the prostrate, dark gray equine. Upon placing his hand behind Smoke's right shoulder, it is obvious that Smoke is still losing blood from the gunshot wound. The size of the brownish-red stain, in the dirt, tells Barton that Smoke is to the point where he cannot afford to expend any more blood and have a chance to live.

"Seth, while I unload the supplies, I need for you to gather as much firewood as you can. When you get that done, take the Morgan horse and go west, on the trail we rode in on. You will find a fresh-water spring just off the trail. Take the canteens and anything else that you can find, and get as much water as you can. I have got to try to get that bullet out of Smoke and get the bleeding stopped. Be quick, but be careful."

While Seth is busy with his essential duties, Barton surveys what medical goods are available in the sack that Wilbur had packed, back in Topeka. Ointment, gauze bandages, strips of cloth for wrapping, and a bottle of whiskey, to act as a disinfectant. All will surely come in handy. Once a fire is started, water can be boiled, and he can sterilize his hunting knife. On the ranch, there are all kinds of minor medical tasks that a person will be called upon to do. But Barton knows he has never come close to attempting what he is facing, and he has never done it on a living creature that means so much to him. And, to add to the challenge,

Barton is not at the top of his physical, or mental, abilities either.

Once Seth gets back with the water, the two combine to get a campfire started. Because Smoke cannot be moved, Barton starts the fire where it can shine the most light upon the patient's wound. Soon, water is boiling on the fire, the hunting knife is resting in the bubbling liquid, gauze and bandages are ready nearby, and the bottle of whiskey will be used later if Barton is successful with removing the bullet and cauterizing the wound. If, being the all-important word as to how this night unfolds.

"Son, I want you to sit back under Smoke's head like you were before. You were doing a good job talking to him, rubbing him, letting him know you are here. If he jerks his head up, try to stay out of the way. If he cries out, just keep talking and rubbing. Just try to remember that we are trying to help him, no matter how bad it may seem on him. Are you ready?"

"Yes, Daddy, let's make Smoke better and go home."

For the next thirty minutes, the emotions swung from hope to frustration, to growing hopelessness. Initially, when Barton would make some headway into following the path of the bullet, Smoke would show signs of discomfort, but would be strong in allowing his traveling partner to continue with the needed probing. But, from time to time, the pain would be too much, causing Smoke to jerk his body and let out a heartbreaking whinny. With each spasm, Barton would lose his place, in the wound tract, and would have to sterilize the knife and start over. Seth was being brave and continued his acts of comfort, even though his young eyes were starting to show signs of weariness.

At some point in the evening, Barton started realizing that he was not adequately equipped, with the medical tools or knowledge, to continue to subject Smoke to further misery. Although he could enter into the wound to where he could feel the bullet grazing the tip of his knife, it was too deep, and he had no way to grip it. To plunge a hunting knife deeper would run the risk of causing blood flow that could not be stopped. So, he pulls out the knife, places it over the fire until it's almost glowing, then quickly inserts it in the wound, cauterizing the damage so that Smoke will lose no more blood. When Smoke hardly moved, or made a noise, from this latest agonizing procedure, Barton knew this was the right, and kindest, thing that could be done.

"Daddy, did you fix Smoke? Is he going to get some relief now?"

Looking at the big gray horse, as it was breathing shallowly and lying quietly, Barton responds, "Yes, Seth. Smoke is finally going to be getting some relief from all of his hurting. Let's take a break, you go lay down and we will see how he is doing in the morning."

It didn't take long for Seth to fall asleep, and Barton has taken his son's place under Smoke's head. He takes his hand and cups it under the horse's chin, an act that the two of them have found to be reassuring and welcoming many times over the years. Barton doesn't even notice his own needs and sufferings now, as his attention is directed upon providing the comfort and peace that the situation now calls for.

"Big gray, I never will forget the morning your momma dropped you on the ground. Once you started coming out, I didn't know when you would finally be done being born. Especially those long legs. I didn't know if you were a great horse or a spider. But I knew you would be special, and you have been, old friend. You have been there through it all, good and bad. You were always there, backing me up. The first day I threw a saddle on you, I promised I would always do the right thing when it came to you. And, as hard as it is to realize what that means, come sunrise, I promise that your suffering will end. One way or another. God doesn't have much to do with me anymore, and I understand that. But I can't help but feel that He can appreciate a good horse. In case I can't get it out, in the morning, thanks for letting me 'ride like the wind', my friend."

For the rest of the night, Barton held Smoke's chin in his hand, while listening to the stallion struggle for his next breath. Any other time, the full moon would be a welcome sight, as it slid across the night sky. But Barton knows what the fleeting luminous globe will give way to in the morning. The tall man is dreading what sunup will bring for his dying friend.

The sun was just peaking over the rugged Kansas horizon when Seth started stirring. He sat up on his bed roll, rubbed the sleep out of his eyes, and looked around. Through the fading darkness of the new dawn, he could see a remnant of the camp-fire still burning, the Morgan horse was standing nearby, Smoke is lying in the same place as last night, and he could see his dad standing over the supine equine. As Seth strained to see what it was that Barton was holding in his hands, his young heart almost stopped when the truth hit him.

Barton was holding his Henry rifle.

"No, Daddy, No! Please, no! Smoke will get better! Please, Daddy, don't!"

"Son, you will understand one day. He could suffer like this for hours or days. The only thing that I can offer him is mercy. Smoke deserves it and I must do it."

"But can't we try again? Can't you ride for help? I will sit with him and talk to him, again."

"Seth, listen to me. I want you to take the Morgan horse and walk to the end of the stone fence. Turn away from this direction, I don't want you to see this. I don't want this to be your last memory of Smoke. Do it, now."

As Seth takes the burly horse, by the reins, and starts walking away, Barton cocks the Henry rifle. With his heart pounding and his eyes swelling, he lifts the long gun to his shoulder and places his trembling finger on the trigger. Closing his eyes to summon whatever last ounce of courage he can to complete this gesture of mercy, Barton lines the sights of the Henry gun up toward its target. Unexpectedly, Barton's concentration is broken by Seth's attempt at getting his father's immediate attention.

"Daddy, why don't you ask them if they can help Smoke?"

Barton, confused and getting agitated, turns to Seth and reprimands him.

"Son, go over there, turn your back, and let me do this, now!"

"But, what if they can help him? Won't you even ask?"

Bordering on exasperation, Barton lowers his rifle, turns to Seth, and exclaims, "What in the hell are you talking about? Who are you talking about, son?"

Lifting his arm and pointing behind Barton, Seth answers, "Them!"

When he follows the direction that the youngest Anderson is pointing, Barton is stunned by what he discovers, standing some two hundred feet away.

Six Indian males, probably Shawnee, in full tribal dress and armament. Barton shakes his head, trying to clear the vision out of his mind. But this is not a hallucination brought on by extreme fatigue and physical injury. This is the real thing standing in front of him.

Could the native way be the last chance for Smoke to survive?

"I sure hope one of you speaks my language, or this is going to get rowdy real fast."

That was the first observation that came out of Barton's mouth, as he surveyed the sight of the natives standing silently before him.

After the young braves looked over the two Andersons, Smoke lying on the ground, and after talking among themselves, one steps forward. By the gathering of feathers and adornments that this one was wearing, Barton surmised that he was a tribal leader, of some sort.

"Yes, Judeahay, I speak your tongue. We do not wish to bring you battle unless that is why you stand there with your long gun."

Barton surveys the other braves, who have not taken their eyes off of him since they arrived. Then, he turns his attention back to the spokesman. Barton lets his Henry rifle slide down, thru his hands, until the butt is resting on the ground. Hopefully, this is interpreted as an act to promote non-aggression.

"No, I do not have the gun raised as a sign of hostility toward you, or your riders. When you walked up, I was in the process of putting this wounded horse out of its pain and misery. If you don't mind, I would like to continue with it."

The supposed tribal leader steps back with the other native males and enters into a discussion that Barton took to be the Shawnee language. During the intense exchange, the principal spokesperson would point at Barton, then point at Smoke, wave his hands in an illustrative manner, and point back toward a waiting Barton. One word kept coming up in the colloquy, and that was 'Judeahay'. Barton had taken notice that this term had been used when the tribal leader had first spoken. After a few more opinions had been shared, or at least that is what Barton figures was happening, the talkative one steps back toward him.

"You must not use your weapon to send your animal out to the spirits, Judeahay. We believe the Shawnee way, before assisting our sacred animal brothers to depart this life, is more just. We will test the wound, then call upon the Great Fathers to decide whether Tonkakee is to continue here, or to be allowed to go run across the high skies."

Barton's mind is spinning, by now. He has gone from the emotional attempt to give Smoke some mercy, to discussing the native ways of dealing with a dying horse. As he gets ready to, politely, tell the head Indian to mind his own business and move on, Seth steps up and asks a forthright question.

"Daddy, I don't understand everything he is saying. But I think he is saying that he might be able to help Smoke. If they can help, doesn't Smoke deserve that chance."

Barton, against what his personal inclinations might be, decides to trust the faith and heart of his son. Walking up to the Shawnee leader, Barton explains, "You do what you think you can do, for the horse. I don't understand it, but I do understand that if that horse is put into any more suffering, or I think you have lost all respect for him, I will put him out of his misery, and will kill anyone who tries to stop me. Do you understand what I have said to you, chief?"

"You are wrong, Judeahay. I am not a chief, for I am Swift Eagle, son of the great chief and warrior Red Hawk, of the Shawnee tribe of the High Plains."

Barton looks Swift Eagle in the eyes, and says, "I don't care who you are, or where you are from. The only thing that I care more about than that gray horse is that young boy right there. If any harm comes to either, I will not hesitate to bring hell down on you and your friends."

"You do not need to worry. For to us, Tonkakee is our great brother. Our hearts and spirits are the same. If his spirit is not to continue to run among the dry land creatures, then we will heed the call of the Great Ones and we will send him on to his life among them."

For the next fifteen minutes, Barton and Seth watch as the Shawnee leader gathers with the other members of the tribal party. One brave, while Barton was discussing the situation with the one who seemed to be in charge, has retrieved their ponies. Swift Eagle reaches inside an ornate leather bag and pulls out items that are hard to distinguish from where Barton sits. A couple of braves retrieve wood to bring the campfire to full flame. During all of this, Smoke has continued to hang on to whatever amount of life that remains in him. Barton maintains his doubt of whether this is the right way to handle this. Seth is just, simply, praying for all his young heart is worth.

When all of the initial preparations seem to be finished, the Indian leader is kneeling beside Smoke, with assorted items laid out beside him. Two braves are sitting by Smoke's head, holding it in a firm, but respectful, way. A duo of braves are kneeling behind Smoke, with their hands upon his side and back, in a purposeful posture to comfort the ailing horse and protect their leader. The sixth is standing by the fire, with containers of water nearby. Barton figures this one is available to go fetch anything that might be needed, whatever that might be.

Whatever doubts Barton may still have, he is drawn into the process of the native ritual of dealing with distressed animals. While five of the braves start a low rhythmic chanting, the leader has taken a flaming branch, out of the fire, and is waving it under a clump of grassy substance that he is holding in his hand. Before long, the greenish substance is smoldering, but not allowed to fully come to an open flame. Once the soddy material is producing a pungent cloud of smoke, Swift Eagle moves it, slowly, back and forth in front of Smoke's nose. Again, Barton wants to jump up and put a stop to this primitive spectacle. But the flicker of hope that Seth is clinging to seems to be influencing Barton's heart, as well. Whatever the purpose of this initial step, Barton notices that Smoke does not seem to be as distressed or laboring for breath.

Next up, after handing the smoking wild grass to one of the braves holding Smoke's head, Swift Eagle reaches into the colorful bag and pulls out a long, slender wand-type item. Barton notices, upon observing it closer, that there seems to be a burr on the tip of it. Once the device has been sterilized in hot water, Swift Eagle places it at the opening of Smoke's bullet wound, gradually working the tool into the injury.

"Daddy, is he hurting Smoke? Is that ok to do?"

"Shhhhh", Barton responded while placing his hand on the worried youngster's shoulder. "He is trying to do what I could not do, and that is get the bullet out of Smoke."

Time passed as Swift Eagle continued to, carefully, work the slender apparatus into the wound tract. Barton could tell, by the expression upon the face of the young brave, that Swift Eagle was making every effort to be effective, without causing discomfort to the unresisting horse. Amazingly, Smoke seems to have been ushered into a docile state by the continuing smoldering clump of mysterious foliage.

As carefully as he, initially, inserted the slim apparatus into Smoke's injury, Swift Eagle starts retracting it, stopping to maneuver it around, as if fishing for something in his great gray patient. Suddenly, Swift Eagle places his left hand against Smoke's side, as he removes the makeshift surgical gadget with his right hand. With great exuberance, he thrusts his left hand in the air, while holding a small item between his thumb and forefinger.

"Tonkakee, Ye-Waugh-Ste! Tonkakee, Ye-Waugh-Ste!"

As Swift Eagle constantly repeats the phrase, while waving his hand over his head, the other braves join in the enthusiasm by echoing the expression. While his fellow Indians continue to indicate their feelings about the state of the situation, Swift Eagle gets up and walks over to where Barton and Seth are sitting. There, the young brave extends his hand, causing Barton to respond in a likewise manner. Into Barton's open palm is placed what Swift Eagle has been clenching between his fingers...a .45 caliber bullet.

Barton examines it, for a moment, and then stands up, faces Swift Eagle, and says the only two words that are needed, at the moment.

"Good enough!"

Seth stares at the bloodstained piece of lead, in his father's hand. Then, the boy looks up at Barton and asks, "Is Smoke going to be ok, now? How long before we can get Smoke up and go on home to Smithview?"

"Well, son," Barton answers, "As far as Smoke being alright, it is still going to take time and care to get him anywhere close to travel ready. But, thanks to getting that slug out of him, Smoke is definitely on the plus side of the scales. And no matter how small that gain is, we will take it, after where we were at a few hours ago."

Swift Eagle, washing the blood from his hands, says, "Judeahay must not move Tonkakee until, at least, two suns and one moon have gone across the sky. We will stay to help with the care of the mighty gray one."

"First thing you are going to do is explain what this 'Judeahay' and 'Tonkakee' talk is all about," Barton proclaims. "I have a feeling that we will have a better understanding of where we stand if we talk in a tongue we both can grasp. I take it that you are referring to me when you use the term 'Judeahay', am I right?"

Swift Eagle explains that Judeahay means 'Shadow Warrior' and is the name that Barton has been given by the Indian nations. The spreading story of the Shadow Warrior has been told around many Indian campfires and hunting parties. The account of how men, with evil spirits, took a man's home tribe from him. Of how the white man's law could not bring rest to the spirits of his fallen ones, so the Shadow Warrior searched until he found those that ambushed his tribe. Once he had released the great thunder from his gun, the Shadow Warrior put the spirits of his home tribe in order and sent the evil ones to their place in the outer darkness. The tribal narrative tells of how Judeahay continues to ride upon the great gray named Tonkakee, which means 'Wind Runner'. Together, they put the spirit world in its natural order by bringing evil men to their ends and giving peace to those who walk among the eternal clans.

Barton just shook his head, amazed that his covert vocation has built such a following among such lots as the newspaper perusers, the saloon yappers, the church gossipers, and now, those who would make him some kind of 'ethereal ghost with a gun' riding a 'mystical mount' in the name of universal peace.

"Well, seeing that we are in the act of speaking where we can understand each other," Barton starts, "I need to make it clear that when the sun is straight above us, there is going to be a bunch of men riding in here, and they are none too happy with me. I had a run-in with them yesterday, I killed three of them and they shot my horse. I can't just leave Smoke for them. I can't and won't. You don't have any reason to stay and fight, and I respect that. At the same time, I would appreciate it if you would take the boy and get him out of here. If you go toward that big butte, off to the northeast, there is a big ranch, three hours on the other side, where you can leave him. The owner is a man named Asa Givens. Tell him you ran into a tall man on a big gray horse, he will know who you are talking about. Tell him the boy is the tall man's son. He will know what to do from there. If you will do that, Swift Eagle, maybe they will start telling stories about you around the council campfires."

"Please Daddy! We can't be split up again. We fought them off before, and we can fight them off again. We can fight for Smoke together, right?"

Barton puts his hand on Seth's trembling shoulder and explains that if neither one of them makes it back to Smithview, then Angus Ford has had the last word on the Anderson family. But, with the help of Jeff and Sally, Seth can keep the family story going, along with the ranch, for years to come.

While Barton tries to console the disheartened youngster, Swift Eagle has been having an active discussion with the other Shawnee braves. Once there seems to be a coming together of viewpoints, Swift Eagle steps over to where Barton and Seth are standing. Upon seeing a chance to start a conversation with Barton, the young brave speaks up.

"I know of this man you call Givens. He is the lord of the land where my people live and hunt. He speaks with straight words and his heart is true. But we will not just take the young one, but we will take you, Judeahay. The dark, dry stains on your shirt, and your mouth, tell that you are broken on the inside. You will be no match, out in the open territory, for any party of attackers. I, and two other braves, will ride with you while one rides fast to tell Givens that we are coming. You, and the young one, will ride the ponies of the two braves who have asked to stay behind to watch over Tonkakee. It will be an honor for them to care for the great Wind Runner."

Barton's facial expression shows that he is having doubts about the Indian leader's plan of handling the situation of an injured man, a seven-year-old, and a recovering equine.

"But, Swift Eagle, two of your braves will not be a match for these violent men. Once they see that your friends are alone, and without any healthy mounts to ride away on, it will only be a matter of time before they are overwhelmed."

Swift Eagle, slightly, tilts his head and smiles, "Oh, but who says that there will be anything to 'see' when the hard riders get here. We have been here, watching you, since last night and you did not know until we walked into your camp. A kibitka sled will be built and Tonkakee will be placed upon it. Your broad horse will be left behind to move the great gray one to a location that only the restless wind, and my braves, will know where he is. The 'medicine grass' will be kept burning and Tonkakee will be still and quiet. Those who chase you will not be willing to waste time on what they thought was a dying horse. Angry white men are predictable that way."

Barton is amused at the comprehension that his new Indian friend seems to have upon the fairer skinned race.

As one of the braves jumps upon his pony and rides in the direction of the Givens ranch, Swift Eagle, and the remaining braves, unload the Morgan horse in preparation for their journey. As few as possible items will be taken with them, as they should make their destination by late evening. A couple of boxes of rifle shells, bandages and water canteens will be the extent of their travel booty.

Barton, and Seth, watch as the Shawnee braves assemble what is called a kibitka sled. Normally, it would be built upon the ground, attached to the towing animal, and then loaded with whatever items were needed to be carried or transported. Because the item to be transported was Smoke, the contraption was assembled around, and under, the large horse. When it was completed and Smoke was securely laying upon it, the braves lifted up one side, and then the other, to a primitive harness device being worn by the Morgan horse. The impromptu setup had been fabricated out of Barton's rope, Smoke's bridle and some other available gear.

Upon being informed that the Shawnee ponies were loaded, and it was time to leave, Barton walks over to where Smoke is laying upon the transport device. It appears that the great animal is not in distress or pain. From time to time, Smoke's right ear would turn outward, as if to let his tall traveling companion know that the big gray was aware of his presence. Placing his hand under Smoke's chin, Barton rubbed gently, and then bent over and spoke softly.

"The last time I had to leave you, when I went to prison, it didn't turn out too bad. But then, I trusted Jeff to take care of you, and for you not to be too much of a pain in the ass. I don't know these young warriors, but I get the feeling that they have a very high opinion of you and that they will take care of you. Again, when you get better, don't be a problem for them. I don't know when I will see you again, big gray, but I will see you again. And, you had better come the first time I whistle for you, Tonkakee."

It had been a long time since Barton had ridden a horse without a saddle. Because of his internal injuries, Barton did not have the option of just hopping up on the Indian pony. While his pride deterred him, for a moment, he placed his foot in the clasped hands of Swift Eagle and was assisted upon his borrowed mount. The same process was followed for getting Seth astride of his pony.

Once everyone was ready to leave, Barton turned around to check on Smoke, one last time. He, somehow, is finding a growing trust in Swift Eagle's plan. The two braves, who were staying behind with Smoke, were already moving the ailing horse to a new location. While one was leading the Morgan horse pulling the kibitka apparatus, the second brave was following with sagebrush to wipe out any footprints or sled tracks that could be followed by the Livingston gang.

"Judeahay, we must get going. We must put distance between us, and this place, before the sun gets overhead."

Barton, until they reach Asa Givens' ranch and safety there, will allow Swift Eagle to be the ramrod of this expedition. He is impressed with the calm foresight and leadership that the young tribal leader has displayed. And now, Barton finds a new way to appreciate Swift Eagle, as Seth is engaging the young Indian leader in a continual conversation about subjects that are, probably, very peculiar and mysterious. But Swift Eagle is giving the younger Anderson his undivided attention and respect.

For the first time in a long time, Barton will just watch and use this time to rest his mind and body. By evening, they will be in a better place, with many more guns on their side.

But Barton will still wonder how Smoke is doing.

12

___

They were about an hour away from the Givens ranch when Barton first noticed the rising dust of a group of riders. If the cloud of dirt had been behind them, then he would have been troubled at the prospects of outrunning, or withstanding, the onslaught of the approaching riders. But, considering that the oncoming horsemen were in front of them, Barton was fairly confident that this was a good thing. When they got closer, Barton could make out that the group of cowboys were being led by an older man, yelling salutations before he could even discern them. But it didn't take too much longer for Barton to recognize the leader of this hard-riding band of protectors.

"You look like a man who could use a glass of Kentucky bourbon and a Cuban cigar. Am I right, Mr. Anderson," yelled Asa Givens, who is being followed by fifteen armed ranch hands?

Barton doesn't feel like yelling his reply back to the old rancher, his insides are on-fire from his injuries and riding on a smaller Indian pony. So he waits until the gathering of cowboys gets closer, and then answers Asa Givens' observation.

"You look like a prosperous rancher who has more to do than ride to the rescue of a busted-up gunslinger."

The old man pulls up beside Barton, extends his hand in a gesture of welcoming, and states, "No matter how big the ranch gets, you never forget your friends and valued acquaintances. When the Indian told us what had happened and who it was, I had so many volunteers I had to make a lot of them stay so the work would get done. Do you want to set up camp and face the spine-less bushwhackers here?"

Barton, enjoying the strong handshake of an honest man who would offer to get involved, answers, "No, if you don't mind, let's try to make it back to your place. The further we can get them from Topeka, the less likely they are to get too bold and arrogant. Plus, it's that much closer to where the boy and I are headed."

"Sounds like a good plan," Givens remarks as he urges his big bay horse near Seth. "And I would guess that this fine lad is the reason for all this fuss? Son, my name is Asa Givens, and it is an honor to meet you!"

Seth grins real big, throws his excited arm out, and says, "My name is Seth Anderson, and it is, equally, my honor to make your acquaintance!"

The old rancher lets out an approving laugh and gives the young boy a hearty handshake. Then, Givens turns back to Barton and explains that the house staff has been given orders to prepare a room for Barton to recover in, have warm food ready and a place for the young guest, too.

"You won't have to worry about anything, while you are with us. You will be taken care of, and the boy will have the run of the ranch. It will be good to have new voices on the place. And, if those bastards from Topeka are stupid enough to come on my ranch and start something, then I hope they kissed anyone who mattered good-bye, because they aren't going to be seeing them ever again."

Barton gets a slight smile, in the corner of his mouth, at the fearless discourse of the old cowpuncher. Then, Barton remembers someone else who will need to be cared for, at some point in the near future.

"I have a rather large, gray friend, out there somewhere, who is going to need to be brought to where he can rest up and recover. I don't suppose that you already have those plans made and in motion, do you?"

Givens' face takes on a look of contemplation and begins, "The Indian told us about what happened to your horse. Sorry to hear about it, he is a good one. I believe that your horse will do better where he is at, for now. One damn thing is for sure, if the Shawnee don't want to be found, the Good Lord will have to take a couple of searches before He will find a trace. Swift Eagle's people come and help us with sick cows and horses. They have some strange ways, but they seem to know what they are doing. They didn't happen to do that bizarre thing with the smoking moss, did they? Whewwww, you got to be careful how close you get to that stuff. It will jumble your mind worse than homemade gooseberry wine."

Barton chuckles, knowing that the old man has, probably, had his share of homemade highly-fermented wine in his lifetime.

"I think we should see about continuing this conversation while we ride to your ranch. Once Livingston's men find out that neither me, nor the boy, are where they left us, they will be headed hard and fast for your place. Swift Eagle made sure to leave some 'easy to follow' tracks to draw them away from the two braves that are staying with Smoke."

"Good thinking," Givens remarked. "You remember my foreman, Carl? Well, while we are riding back, he will be getting the rest of the men armed and stationed. We moved the livestock, before we left, so that any fighting would be between the 'two-legged' species. Don't mean any disrespect, Swift Eagle, but I have had the pleasure of kicking a lot of backsides that tried to come up against the ranch, both of the white and red varieties."

Swift Eagle laughs, and retorts, "Yes, old cattleman. But the Shawnee nations sing songs of when the great warrior chief, Red Hawk, could still put fear in the hearts of white men by putting on the war paint and riding into their camps. I bet you spilled your whiskey because he made your hands tremble when you heard he was in the territory. Right, old Indian fighter?"

"My, oh my, Swift Eagle," the elder cowboy reflected. "Your daddy, Red Hawk, was one of the fiercest fighters out of the Indian lands. I never wanted to tangle with him, and was always glad to see him ride away. To this day, there is no white man that I count it more of an honor to sit with than I do when I am at the campfire of Red Hawk. Barton, when we get you healed up and these pecker-heads from Topeka are taken care of, I will have to take you up to the Shawnee camp and introduce you to a real warrior."

Swift Eagle lifts his hand, in a sign of respect to the old rancher, pulls his pony out of the procession and rides in the direction of the North Plain, where his father and the Shawnee tribe are located. With Barton and Seth in the safe hands of Givens, and his riders, the young son of the mighty Indian chief will check on Tonkakee and his caretakers. Once this is accomplished, Swift Eagle will head to the Shawnee camp to spend a few moments with his family, before returning to the Givens' place. Watching Barton and Seth interact has made the young father anxious to speak of his adventures, so far, with Little Hawk.

Barton does not hear the bantering of any of the men around him, as his mind is on a more intimate subject, Seth. The shrouded sentiments of being a father are feverishly trying to crawl out of the dormant place in his darkened heart. As he watches his young son chatting with the ranch hands, as they ride back to the Givens' spread, his memory jumps past the last year of tragedies to a more heartfelt base of reference, when Jenny was still alive. Barton thinks of how proud she would be of how Seth has endured his trials and tests, and how he has let them make him more mature and not break him. Barton, even, catches himself imagining Seth, and Adam, helping with the ranch chores, driving cattle, and just having father-son talks as they ride across the Kansas landscape. But Barton will not let himself stay in that place of vain wishes and futile fantasies.

As they rode up to the main estate, of the Givens' ranch, Barton can't detect any special preparations that have been made for any potential onslaughts that are being anticipated. But, slowly, ranch hands start appearing from behind wagons, stacks of logs, out of barns and corrals. Each man armed and ready for any conflict that the Topeka riders might bring down upon them. After welcoming back their fellow workmen, the cowboys make a circle around the old rancher, in anticipation of what plans were to be shared for the evening.

"Everyone back to your assigned positions," Givens' voice thunders over the gathering. "Each post will be manned by two men, one will stand watch while the other gets their meal or rests, but both will be ready if an attack comes. We don't know when they will come or how they will come, but we are going to be ready to send the bastards packing with bitter remembrances of their first visit to the Givens ranch. They are coming for the boy, but they will leave with their asses in their hands!"

The assembly of cowboys, and ranch workers, start yipping,

yelling and waving their hats in the air, as they react to the old man's confident declaration.

"Glad to see you and the boy, big man."

Barton turns to acknowledge the salutation and finds Carl, the ranch foreman, standing by the Pinto pony that Barton is riding. He nods his head as Carl tips his hat to Seth, who returns the act with a big smile and a nod of his young head. Like father-like son, the foreman thinks as all the riders start dismounting from their horses and ponies.

Givens puts his hand upon the shoulder of Barton and informs him to take Seth inside the big ranch house. For now, there is no reason for Barton to take a position among the others. The priority is for the Anderson duo to clean up, eat a good hot meal, and to get some rest. The staff is prepared to wait upon their every need. Barton likes the sound of that, but he cannot rid himself of the feeling that they have not avoided a confrontation with Livingston's outfit, especially with the one called Hartmann. Barton has encountered gunmen like this one, and he knows that he humiliated the hired shooter in their last confrontation. Hartmann had to go back to Topeka, with his tail between his legs, and Barton knows that all rules of engagement would be off now. It will be dirty, it will get bloody, and it won't be about getting Seth back, but it will be about getting Hart-mann's pride and reputation back. Barton wishes they would come now, while Livingston's assassin is filled with rage, for that is when these types will make their biggest mistakes and falter. But, no matter when it starts, Barton is prepared to end this, once and for all.

It wasn't long after they had eaten that Seth fell asleep upon a big, plush couch in the house's library. Givens instructs the nearby Indian valet to pick up the boy and take him to an awaiting bed upstairs. The ranch owner then steps over to an oaken cabinet, opens it, and pulls out two glasses and an unopened bottle of Kentucky bourbon. After pouring and handing his guest one glass, he fills one for himself and sits down across from Barton. Each man takes a slow sip of the smooth, distilled potation and waits for a conversation to commence. It was soon after the second sip that Givens spoke up.

"The last time you were here, you were looking for a cur named Coy Newton. He was one of the cretins that murdered your family. I, later, heard reports that you had caught up with him in Prestonburg and you had killed him. How did it feel to put a bullet in that son-of-a-bitch? I never got the chance to serve justice on the scum that killed Aylen, my Rose of the Ranch. Right or wrong, I always felt like it would bring me a sense of satisfaction to watch them bleed out in front of me. I know she didn't die quickly, and I would have wanted to milk their demise for every drop of benefit that it could offer. I know that sounds pretty sad, doesn't it?"

Barton thinks for a moment, takes another sip of the Kentucky liquor, then he looks the old rancher in the eye and responds.

"No, it's not sad. I lived with that thought for a long while. It's what drove me to get up each day, to breath each second, to want to live another moment. But it's an empty pursuit that offers nothing in return. It's a hollow dream that is void of a satisfactory outcome. I look back on that day in Prestonburg and realize how ignorant it was to take on three men who were fortified in a bank building. Yes, I killed them. But if I had been killed I would have never known I had a son out there somewhere. Losing my loved ones killed something inside me, made me do things that I will have to live with for the rest of my life, and I will never be the man I was before that morning in Smithview. But, upstairs in your guest room, is a chance for me to try to become something, if not for anyone else, at least to him. Because I was driven by hate and rage, I will always have to carry a gun and be a reason for outlaws to look over their shoulders. And I will do it without reservation or consideration. But there is one other thing I get to always be, and that's a father to Seth."

Givens' face takes on a softer expression, and then he lifts his bourbon glass, in Barton's direction, and says.

"Thank you, cowboy. I will always miss my Rose of the Ranch, but I will keep Aylen alive with the picture over the fireplace and the memories in my old heart. I say let's toast the fact that we were lucky men to have such wonderful women to hold and to love."

Barton lifts his glass to Givens and says what he would normally say in these situations.

"Good enough."

Barton never got the rest that Givens, and the house staff, had prepared for him. If he wasn't anticipating the sounds of gunfire to start filling the night air, at any moment, he was thinking about how Smoke was doing. Even though he tried to think of alternative approaches to handle the situation, Barton knew that leaving Smoke with the Shawnee braves was the only way to get Seth away from where they confronted Hartmann, and give Smoke a chance to recover. But, whether it was pursuing outlaws, making camp in the wide Kansas prairies, or hunting a ten-point buck deer, he always felt better when he knew the big gray horse was nearby.

All was quiet at the Givens ranch until around four in the morning came. Barton noticed a horse came running up to the big house. Almost immediately after, raised voices could be heard in a mixture of English and Shawnee dialect. When the voices got loud and bordered on out of control, Barton would hear the old rancher yell for all to shut up. After a temporary pause in the heated debate, the conversation would pick up in pace, volume and intensity, causing Givens to have to demand calm and order in the fevered discussion.

While Barton was trying to make out what the impassioned squabble was all about, he heard another noise that got his attention, for the moment. As he looks thru the dimly lit room, he can make out Seth coming down the stairs from the second floor of the big house. The young boy was rubbing his eyes as he searched out for his father.

"Daddy, what is all the yelling about? What are they so upset about?"

Barton walks over to Seth, puts his hand on his youthful shoulder, and answers," I don't know, but you wait here. I am going to go find out, right now."

Before he could turn and head to the front door, Givens, Carl and a brave, that Barton recognizes as one of the Shawnee warriors that stayed with Smoke, come walking into the library. Even though the big room was darkened, he could see enough to know that something wasn't right by the looks on their faces.

"White Bear says that the hired gun, that you talked about, went crazy when he saw that you and the boy were gone. This brave, and the other one who stayed behind, watched from their hiding place. The gunslinger didn't follow the tracks that Swift Eagle had laid out. Seems there was an Apache tracker with them, and he found signs that Shawnee braves had been in the area. The one you call Hartmann, and twelve ginned-up riders, headed in the direction of the Shawnee camp on the north part of my ranch. White Bear followed behind them. My word, Anderson! They rode in with their guns blazing, not caring what they hit or who they hurt. The tribe, thinking it was riders from my ranch to help with the fall buffalo hunt, were caught totally off-guard. It's bad, real bad!"

Barton walks over to where his Henry rifle is leaning up against the wall, picks it up, jerks the lever action down and up, then turns to Givens. From the look on Barton's face, the old rancher starts shaking his head, in a negative way, and starts pleading with the tall man.

"Oh, hell no. You are in no shape to ride anywhere, let alone take on an army of paid thugs. Put the gun down and stay here with your boy. We will ride to the Shawnee camp, see what the damage is, and then come back here to figure where to go from there."

While Barton is checking his saddle bag to see if he has his usual staples for what he has in mind, White Bear starts talking with Carl, the foreman. Again, the changing look on the lead cowpuncher's face tells Barton that the next news is not going to be any easier to swallow that what has been shared, so far.

Barton steps up to the ranch foreman and calmly, but firmly asks, "What did the Indian tell you?"

Carl replies, "Chief Red Hawk is dead. The old warrior wasn't going to let anyone tear thru his tribe without some response. The one you call Hartmann emptied his gun into the chief, as the old Indian chief laid helpless on the ground. Swift Eagle was shot upon returning to the camp. Whether the chief's son is alive is anyone's guess. Other braves were shot, beaten and humiliated in front of the women. Then, they attacked the squaws in a way that women should not be treated."

Barton continues to watch Carl, getting a feeling that the ramrod has not shared everything that the Shawnee messenger has told him.

"Carl, now isn't the time to hold anything back, He told you something that you are hesitant to tell me. What is it that you are keeping from me? Tell me, now!"

The ranch foreman takes a big breath, looks at Givens for approval and gets it with a nod of the ranch owners head toward Barton.

"They took Swift Eagle's boy, Little Hawk. He is about three years old, I guess. Took him out of his mother's arms as she was screaming for them to leave him alone. The professional gunman pistol whipped her and left her on the ground, next to Red Hawk's dead body. White Bear was instructed to give you a message, "come to the Livingston estate with your boy, come alone, and come unarmed. Then, and only then, will the redskins get the kid back."

Everyone in the room watches Barton, waiting for a reaction, a word, a sign that would suggest what he is thinking, what he is planning, what he is ready to do. Barton takes a few steps in Seth's direction, gets down on one knee, looks the youngster in the eyes, and unswervingly speaks, father to son.

"It will be a cold day in hell before I take you back to anyone, or go unarmed anywhere."

Seth, giving his dad a look that could only be interpreted as being peeved, says, "That little boy has been taken away from his family, just like I was, hasn't he?"

"Yes, son. Because the Shawnee were willing to help you, Smoke and I, when we were in trouble, they have now been hurt because of it. And, like you, the little boy needs help to get away from Livingston. I think I have to go and be whatever help I can be, to get Swift Eagle's son back. You alright with that?"

"Daddy, if you promise that when you come back that me, you and Smoke can, finally, go home to the ranch."

Barton, sensing his son's tottering support for this new cause, puts his calloused palm against Seth's face and says, "Yes, we will go home to Smithview, I promise."

Seth puts his young arms around Barton, tightly squeezes and then softly asks, "Do you think it would be alright if I pray for Swift Eagle's son, his tribe and pray for you?"

Barton looks down at the younger Anderson, who is looking up and waiting for an answer to his heartfelt inquiry.

"Yes, Seth. You pray for all of us. We are going to need all the help we can get."

13

"He's not as fast as that big stallion that you ride, but I damn sure wouldn't want to live on the difference, that's for sure."

Asa Givens was talking about the buckskin horse that Barton would be riding to the Shawnee camp. The horse's official breeder's name was 'Kingmaker's Delight', but the elder ranch owner had nicknamed him 'Jake' in honor of his late brother, who helped start the Givens' ranch many years ago. Barton threw his saddle bag across the hind quarters of the borrowed steed, slid his Henry rifle into an attached sheath, and then got up on the impressive horse. At first, it was a strange feeling, for he hadn't sit in another saddle, or upon another horse, since Smoke was first broke to ride. Initially, Jake seemed to have some 'getting acquainted' anxiety, but it wasn't long until the big buckskin was ready to go.

"You, Carl and fifteen men head to Swift Eagle's camp." Givens started. "You can ride faster and farther without me along. Later, I am sending the Shawnee house staff on, in a buckboard wagon. They deserve to be with their people during this time. There will be more supplies coming with them, for the tribal people and for whatever plans you have about getting that boy back. Do you have any ideas about what you are going to do, when you get to Topeka?"

Barton, spins Jake around to where the horse is facing Givans, and wryly answers.

"Going to find Livingston, shoot that son-of-a-bitch between the eyes, get Swift Eagle's son back, kill anyone who tries to stop me and return here in time to have that Cuban cigar you owe me."

"Dang, man," Givens retorts! "You are pretty confident in that gun of yours, aren't you?'

Barton pulls his Colt revolver from its holster, gives the cylinder a spin, and replies, "The gun has nothing to do with it. Most guns have the same number of bullets, same caliber, same barrel length. The difference is in the fact I have already beat Livingston and Hartmann, and that galls them. I use my gun to pay a debt I owe to society, Hartmann uses his to cover that he is just a blowhard, and Livingston buys other men's guns to cover that he is a coward. If this goes bad, it won't be because they are that good, it will mean that I wasn't prepared. Make no mistake, I am prepared to kill all of them or die trying. They may be ready to kill me, but I am sure that they are not ready to die to do it. And that will be my advantage. Fear of dying has killed many a man."

Givens reaches up his hand, which is met by Barton's matching gesture. After a strong grip and shake, the long-time rancher smiles, and says, "Oh man, what I wouldn't give to be a few years younger and more nimble. I would love to ride with you, Mr. Anderson. One thing you won't have to worry about is the well-being of Seth. The only way anyone will ever get that boy off of this ranch is for there to be no one standing. I know my men, and they will fight for what is right, and I am pretty sure that boy is worth them dying for!"

"Good enough!", Barton responds.

Around an hour and a half later, Barton, Carl and the Givens riders could see the smoke rising from the Shawnee camp, even when they were still a mile away. Upon seeing the tepees burning all around them, as they entered the tribal site, their senses were soon drawn to the sound of crying, and grieving. Barton's ire was raised at the sight of young native girls holding their dead warriors, one child holding it's lifeless mother, and the severely injured who were just lying in the dirt with no one to hold them.

Barton pulled back on Jake's reins, causing the buckskin horse to stop. Carl, and the other ranch riders followed his action, dismounted and started looking for someone that they could help, or at least cover, until other arraignments can be made.

"Find someone who knows where Swift Eagle is," Barton says to Carl. "You can speak the language and they know you. I am afraid the only thing that I can offer them is my gun and the temperament to get them some retribution for this travesty."

Carl asks a couple of members of the tribe where the son of Red Hawk is. Then, the ranch foreman returns to Barton, who is kneeling while pulling a deer skin over the lifeless body of a young brave, while his apparent mother cries out, in her grief.

"The one squaw says that Swift Eagle is seeing to his wife's injuries, over by that stand of willows. Being the chief now, with the death of Red Hawk, he will have to make arraignments for the body of his father to be placed upon his honored death scaffold, in the burial grounds, before the sun sets."

Barton stands, touches the brim of his hat in respect for the fallen native warrior, then heads in the direction of the large grove of willows. Once there, he finds Swift Eagle treating the brutal lacerations upon his wife's face, left there by the pistol whipping that Hartmann had given her. Upon closer observation, Barton can see fresh blood running down the side of the young brave.

"How bad are you shot," Barton asks Swift Eagle, as he continues to give medical aid to his injured, and disoriented, wife?

"Not so bad that I can't ride to Topeka and deal with the white man that killed my father, beat my woman and stole my son," answered the new chief of the Shawnee High Plains tribe. "I have spent many moons telling my father that we must find peaceful ways to live among the whites, but he would tell me that the white man's words may change, but their hearts never will. Today, I am sorry I did not listen to the mighty Red Hawk, for I must send him to the Great Fathers, with the honor he deserves. As for me, I must hang my head, in dishonor, for not listening to the words of great wisdom that I was given."

Barton listens to the young chief, knowing it wasn't that long ago that the same feelings were running thru his mind, heart and soul after losing his family to evil-hearted men. Barton reaches into his pocket, pulls out a clean handkerchief and hands it to Swift Eagle to use to clean the wounds of his impaired spouse, pained by her wounds and the taking of their child.

"I know you are hurting and angry," Barton starts. "I have been where you are, and I have felt the hate that is gripping your heart. But look behind you and you will see sixteen men caring for your injured and dead, putting out the fires of your teepees, ready to ride upon those who did this to your tribe. If you look real close, you will notice they are all white men. Don't make the mistake I made, don't lump the few lying bastards in with the good men. Men like Asa Givens, who didn't have to send these men here. He doesn't have to care, but he does care, and they are here."

Swift Eagle finishes cleaning his wife's face, then painfully lifts himself up, turns to Barton and entreats the tall man standing by him, "Will Judeahay help me put the wandering spirits of my people at harmony with those in the next world? My father can no longer ride with me, for he sleeps and waits for someone to make things right. I am the chief of my people now and they look to me to lead them out of this time of great shame and degradation. The glory of our fathers has been taken and will not return until we display our battle faces and show that we are worthy to possess it again. Will the Shadow Warrior ride with the Shawnee, or is he just the white man's avenging champion?"

Barton, resolutely, responds, "First, I suggest that you do what needs to be done to give your father and your people a mannerly sendoff. Then, I say we ride to Topeka, kill some worthless white men, and get your boy back."

For the next few hours, Carl and half of the Givens ranch hands cut down young trees to be fashioned into burial scaffolds, upon which Red Hawk, and the other victims of the Hartmann attack, will be laid. The Shawnee women prepare the bodies to be placed upon their resting places of peace and honor. The other ranch workers toil, together with the Shawnee braves, to salvage what teepee makings can be redeemed and assembled into shelters for the wounded to be placed in. Barton, at the request of Swift Eagle, takes this time to rest and prepare for what will come later. He is sensing the tribe is putting its hopes in the 'Shadow Warrior' to bring some sort of native magic to the rescue effort. Barton, simply, knows he must be at his best when the Livingston bunch is confronted and the only wizardry he will bring will be in the form of a Henry rifle and a Colt sidearm.

The sun heads toward the Kansas horizon as the funeral arraignments are being finished. The wooden edifices upon which the bodies of Red Hawk, and other casualties of the Livingston assault, have been erected and they reach high toward the cloudless sky. Red Hawk is dressed in full adornment, fitting of the status of which he held. The once great Indian leader will be supplied with full headdress, tribal necklace, knife and bow that he might be received, by the Great Fathers, into the next life prepared to take his place as a spirit leader to the Shawnee nation.

Out of respect, Barton will not attend the burial ceremony. He has traveled enough, read enough and has a sense that this is not the time for him, Carl or the other ranch hands to breach the tribal sanctity and sacredness of the burial grounds, nor the mystical customs of laying natives into their final place of repose.

As Barton checks the saddle on Jake, and does an inventory of the supplies in his saddle bag, Carl walks over by him. Not a word is shared as the two men stand and listen to the rhythmic beating of the drums and the impassioned chants of Swift Eagle and the tribal elders as they voice their calls to release the spirits of the departed that they might transition to what awaits them. The native women perform their roles, in the ceremony, by crying out their grief mantras to announce to the awaiting guardians that the souls of their loved ones will be arriving into their supernatural destinies soon.

"Whether you understand it or not," Carl observes, "you have to admire how much they seem to believe in the whole thing of spiritual fathers, sacred lands and whatever is out there waiting for them. What do you think about it all, Anderson?"

Barton, continuing to restock his saddle bag, remarks without looking up at the ranch foreman.

"I guess everyone has to believe in something, or maybe you don't. Doesn't matter to me."

"Don't you believe in something, big man? A higher power, a great spirit being that controls everything, that has his eyes on everything. I guess what those Indians are doing, right now, is not a lot different than what white people do on Sunday mornings. Instead of drums, white people have pianos or other instruments. In place of the chanting, we have songbooks and singing. We even dress our dead up, as if they are going to some big party or encounter, just like they fancy their dead up. When you think about it, the methods may be different, but the purpose may not be so different between the white man and the red man. Don't you think so, Anderson?"

Barton closes the flap on his saddle bag, pulls his Colt from its holster, and says, "I believe in the things that keep me alive. Like keeping my gun loaded, the sights set true and the ability to clear leather faster than the person I am facing. Falter in any one of those and it don't matter what you believe in, you are going to be just as dead."

The tribal funeral observance comes to a conclusion about two hours after it began. Darkness is spreading across the Kansas plains as Swift Eagle, White Bear and the others come out from the sacred place of final rites and resting. Barton will not say anything, in this moment, as to let the young chief be in the lead of any initial thoughts, plans or actions. It is in these beginning stages of his fledgling status, as new tribal chieftain, that the Shawnee nation will form their trust, respect and loyalty to his leadership. Barton will not let the mystical dimension of the 'Shadow Warrior' eclipse the real positional authority that Swift Eagle now possesses. Barton knows that Judeahay is just a transcendental figure in their active minds, but the young chief will be in front of his people as long as the

Great Fathers decide that it should be, according to Shawnee folklore.

"My father, and the others, are now on their journey to an abundant land of wild game, clear rivers and battle stories. I am ready to make new victory stories, and the first one will be getting my son back from those hired riders who took him and the pride of my people."

Carl steps up to Swift Eagle, and says, "I have fifteen armed men that are willing to ride with your braves to Topeka. Mr. Givens has sent us enough ammo and supplies to fight until we get Little Hawk back from the Livingston raiders. With Anderson alongside us, that should be plenty of firepower to overwhelm their forces, retrieve the young boy and let the world know that the Shawnee are still a powerful people and capable of taking care of their own. Isn't that right, cowboy?"

Barton says nothing as he continues to check his saddlebags, guns and the cinch straps on Jake's saddle. When his new friend offers no suggestions or confirmations, Swift Eagle walks over to where Barton is standing and studies him until Barton looks at the young chief. Then, with his eyes locked on Barton's face, in an attempt to read his mind, Swift Eagle probes what thoughts are running through the Shadow Warrior's mind, as pertaining to the next moves that should be made.

"Judeahay, you do not say anything when the ranch boss asks for your support or opinion. Are you having second thoughts about riding with Swift Eagle and the Shawnee war party? Are you not able to ride and fight now? Are your guns too weak and their thunder too quiet to attempt such a ride for my son and the honor of the High Plains natives? Maybe the Shadow Warrior is just that, a shadow in the minds of silly, simple Indians that tell stories until they grow beyond the truth. Are you Judeahay, or are you just a ghost, an echo with no real substance?"

Barton waits to respond, for he knows that Swift Eagle is hurting, physically and emotionally. When Barton realizes that the young tribal leader is still staring at him, waiting to have his anguished qualms reassured, he resolutely begins his response to the awaiting young chief.

"I didn't ask to be some spiritual hallucination to your people, or anyone. I am just a man who killed the people who came and raided my homeplace and murdered my family. That's it, that's all. I am not some 'supernatural ghost with a gun' that is capable of feats beyond human limitations. I shoot fast, I shoot straight, I shoot without hesitation. That is what has got me this far. I said I would ride with you, and I said we would kill the men who did these things. And I will fight until we get your boy back or my gun is laying in the dirt with my dead hand still holding it. That is all I can offer you. No tricks, no magic, no mystical powers. Just a rifle, a sidearm and two fists to fight until there is no need to fight anymore."

Swift Eagle reaches out and takes Barton by the forearm, grips it firmly, and replies, "For tonight, the High Plains natives will not ride with the Shadow Warrior. We will have the honor to ride with someone far greater and far more preferred, our friend and brother, Anderson."

Barton returns the assuring grip of Swift Eagle's forearm and nods his head, in agreement.

"Alright, cowboy," Carl starts. "What part of the plan does not meet with your approval? If we don't have enough ranch hands, I can send someone back to get more guns and men from Mr. Givens' place. The young chief can probably send word for more Shawnee braves, from other camps, to join in this endeavor to make things right."

Barton looks out over the Kansas prairie, noticing that a new Harvest moon is settling into its place in the distant night sky. He thought it ironic that the natives mark time in 'the number of moons' that pass. And he knows that a desperate Livingston will not wait very many 'moons' before he takes drastic steps to settle the situation at the Livingston estate. Barton knows this could mean using Little Hawk as a bargaining piece, or as a shield from the guns of awaiting law officers. If they wait too long, or act too quick, the Shawnee child may not have many 'moons' left.

Barton takes a long, deep breath, then turns to the ranch foreman and answers, "I have no doubt that we have some of the finest cowboys and braves that could be called upon. I am sure they are strong, gutsy and can shoot with the best of anyone. But, I have been to the Livingston estate. He may be an idiot when it comes to hiring those to protect him, but he wasn't a fool when it came to constructing a stronghold to provide refuge in. Anyone who rides hellbent for a shoutout will get that boy killed before they can touch the outer walls. I have been told that an assembly of marshals and soldiers have been sitting, for days, with no way to get in without causing tragic loss of innocent lives inside. This is going to take a different approach, something that they didn't see coming. It is going to need to be a case of 'distracting and concealing', with a little 'shocking' thrown in, for good measure. And it can't be done with a thundering force riding up on them."

Carl, with a puzzled look on his face, asks, "What do you have in mind, cowboy?"

Barton turns to Swift Eagle, gets a slight smile on his face and replies, "I had a very sharp Indian brave tell me that he could hide a wounded horse to where no one could see it, even if they were standing near it. I don't know how yet, but I think we might be able to get in Livingston's big house, find Little Hawk and get the boy in a safe place. All under Livingston's arrogant nose so he doesn't see what's coming until it's too late."

Swift Eagle, looking more confident with the aspects of

riding with Barton, inquires, "You do not have the plan of how to get Little Hawk away from Livingston, but do you know how many it will take to perform this act of 'distracting and concealing' on the rich man's hired guns?"

Barton replies, "My gut is telling me four. Me, you, White Bear and a U.S. marshal friend who is already there. Plus, if needed, a couple of new acquaintances who I am sure will be more than willing to help with the distraction part."

Carl protests, "You have got to be crazy! Four of you facing over thirty hired guns in a fortified position? Cowboy, I have fifteen good men, who are armed and ready to ride. Just give us the word."

Barton walks over to Carl, lightly taps the ranch foreman on the chest with his fist, and remarks, "I am counting on that. Instead of going to Topeka, you will be of better use back at the Givens ranch. If this doesn't go well, and by some stretch of the odds we don't make it, then I will die knowing that Seth has all of you looking out for him. Protect my boy, Carl, if Hartmann or anyone comes after him."

Carl nods his head, to the affirmative, and tells the ranch riders to mount up and head back to the Givens' place.

Barton, Swift Eagle and White Bear take little time to load up for their journey to Topeka. They will ride all night, under the illumination of the brilliant harvest moon. Ammo, weapons, water and a few food staples will be all that they will need for this undertaking. When the unlikely trio gets ready to mount up, Swift Eagle inquires...

"Anderson, can you think of anything else that we will need, or you would like to take to Topeka with us?"

Before he can answer, Barton hears a sound that causes his heart to leap in his chest and puts an unexpected smile on his face. He shakes his head as he turns to see where the familiar whinny is coming from.

It was Smoke, standing about fifty yards away.

Barton, still finding it arduous to find his breath, walks toward his big gray friend. Although Smoke was trying to come closer to the approaching ally, it was plain to see that the effort was hampered by a pronounced limp. Barton reaches out his hand, meeting the great equine with a rub on the chin and a playful scratching of the ears.

"Hey, big guy! Good to see you."

Smoke makes a long, neighing sound, as if to return his pleasure in seeing his long-time travel companion. As the two continue to enjoy this reunion, Swift Eagle smiles and says, "I think Tonkakee is wanting to go with us. What do you think, Anderson?"

Barton, continuing to hold Smoke's chin in his hand and looking over the mighty animal, replies, "Love to have you with us, big guy. But not until you are ready to be the 'Wind Runner' again. You stay here and get better. Soon, you and I will go get Seth, and go home to Smithview, finally."

Smoke throws his head up and down, in more of an act of protest than agreement. Even though his body might be healing, the heart of the great stallion is still full of fight and fury.

After a last rub of Smoke's chin, Barton walks back to Jake, gets upon the big buckskin horse and joins Swift Eagle and White Bear as they leave for the long night's ride to Topeka.

14

———

Riding under the Harvest moon made traveling easier across the Kansas landscape. There was not a lot of conversation between the three riders. Other than an occasional dialogue between Swift Eagle and White Bear, in their Shawnee dialect, each man seemed to be willing to give solitary space to the other two. Barton was totally invested in devising a plan that would give them a chance to rescue Little Hawk, even though the odds seemed to grow against their success the closer they got to Topeka. Swift Eagle thought of what his father, Red Hawk, would do to rescue his grandson and namesake. Would the great Indian chief trust a white man, the way that Swift Eagle is putting all hope of seeing his son in the hands of the one the Shawnee call 'Judeahay'? White Bear was just searching deep inside himself, hoping he was worthy of the confidence that his young chief, and the tall cowboy, seemed to be putting in him.

When they were a mile from the city limits of Topeka, as daybreak was spreading across the prairie horizon, they encountered another piece of Barton's rescue plan to get Little Hawk. Although Swift Eagle and White Bear had their hands upon their weapons, prepared to react to any unexpected circumstances, Barton knew who the approaching rider was. This unexpected meeting will save Barton from having to locate the fourth man of this unusual quartet of redeemers.

"Well, gunslinger, I always hoped that Smoke would get smart and leave you walking," Marshal Tomes proclaimed, trying not to crack up at his facetious observation.

Barton, not wanting the federal lawman to get in the best dig, responded, "No, he actually heard that we were going to have to put our lives in your hands, and he took off running, in the other direction. May be the fastest I have ever seen him move. Just had no faith in you, at all, law dog!"

Tomes pulls Hickory up next to the buckskin that Barton is riding and extends his hand in an act of greeting a trusted friend. After Barton matches the gesture, he introduces the marshal to the two Indian riders with him.

"I heard about your father, Swift Eagle," Tomes shares. "Red Hawk was a respected chief to the state and federal governments. A lot of lives have been saved, on both sides, due to your father's wisdom and guidance. It is, truly, a loss for the Shawnee nation and for the white man's world, too."

Swift Eagle stares at Tomes, emotionless, and answers, "The mighty chief, Red Hawk, would not have let his grandson be taken by white devils. Especially, when my father was strong and open-eyed. Now, my son is in the hands of a white man who considers a child to be no more than a possession to be traded or sacrificed. Your law did nothing to keep my son safe, so the Shawnee code will guide my way and my weapons now. Are you here to ride with us or against us? Your answer will decide where the sights of my guns are aimed, government man!"

The marshal looks at Barton, who gives Tomes a look that,

pretty much, states where the man on the buckskin horse stands in this matter. Tomes then turns back to Swift Eagle, takes a moment to capture his thoughts and words, and then starts...

"I will do everything that I can to help get your son back, I promise you that. Where you are directed by the ancient Shawnee traditions and ways, I must honor the laws and ways of my people, my government. Our laws did not keep Livingston's hired guns from taking your son and hurting your people, I admit that. While they are not perfect, our laws give us a road to travel, a way of doing things, that gives us control, stability and direction in how to handle many things that we encounter. The fact that you are willing to ride with this man gives me hope that we can get your son back, in a way that will be best for many and profitable for all. I do not agree with all of the ways Barton approaches things, but I can live with the results that he gets, more times than not."

Swift Eagle turns and looks at Barton, who gives the young chief a look that says this man, with the star on his chest, can be trusted. After looking up at the dawning sky, taking a deep breath and releasing it sharply, Swift Eagle gives his attention back to Tomes and asks.

"The one you call 'Barton' says he is willing to kill every man that has played a part in taking Little Hawk. Will you? Or does the metal trinket, on your shirt, make you worthless, when the time comes for dues to be paid. Can I trust you to avenge Red Hawk and my people?"

Tomes, feeling that the moment has come to put all the cards on the table, answers with an unwavering commitment, "I will kill any man that attempts to shoot anyone who is trying to return your son to you, and your people. No questions, no reservations. But I will not take any chance of other innocent people becoming casualties in this operation. You watch my back, I will watch yours, and together we will make this work and we all go home to those who are waiting."

Swift Eagle looks at Barton, who is sitting on Jake, his arms folded, his face expressionless, not offering the young Shawnee leader any indications of how the unseasoned chief should proceed from this moment in their journey.

"You, Anderson, want this man to go with us to get Little Hawk? You trust his gun and his heart?"

Barton looks at Tomes, gets a little smirk in the corner of his mouth, then turns back to the awaiting Swift Eagle.

"Right now, I would want no one else. He has held my life in his hands, more than once. And yet, here I sit today. Yes, Swift Eagle, I trust his gun. But I trust his words and his heart even more."

Swift Eagle directs his pony next to Hickory, extends his hand toward Tomes, and says, "The word of Anderson is strong for me. The chief of the High Plains Shawnee pledges that I will have your back until we can share a pipe around the tribal fire of my people!"

As the marshal and the native leader shake hands, in commitment to the cause, Barton jerks on Jake's reins, causing the big buckskin to spin in his tracks. As he presses his heels into the sides of Jake, Barton expresses two words that are sufficient for the moment...

"Sounds good!"

The first stop, for the newly banded quartet of riders, was the office of Rand Cannon's shipping company. Rand, and Wilbur, played a big part in getting Barton into the Livingston estate, the first time. This time, things are more combustible, and Barton is not sure if the cargo haulers will be receptive to being involved in an operation that is sure to involve gunfire, people getting hurt and, possibly, worse. But once they arrived and it was shared that a child had been taken, Rand was immediately on-board. Even though it took a little more persuasion, Wilbur was also ready to do his part.

So, with all the players present and accounted for, Barton started telling of an idea to get Little Hawk to safety and out of Livingston's grip. Rand and Wilbur would be in charge of the distraction. White Bear would be the one to act as the 'ghost' who finds a way to get over the wall and into the mansion without detection. Once the young brave is inside, he was to locate Little Hawk and procure a safe place for both of them. Once White Bear has given a signal that he and the young Shawnee boy are secure, the rescue effort will begin with Barton, Tomes and Swift Eagle moving as quickly as possible into the mansion. There will be one strategy, and only one, when they make their initial onrush...shoot to kill. Barton is betting on all innocent servants and staff to seek cover and not being loyal to Livingston. Anyone moving toward the advancing trio will, surely, be coming to stop them. With Little Hawk and White Bear out of the line of fire, that will be an aspect that won't have to worried about, when the shooting starts.

"There are almost forty marshals, deputies and soldiers surrounding the estate's walls, prepared to engage the Livingston crew. Wouldn't you want to take advantage of all of those guns?" Tomes asks, not wanting Barton to think the lawman is doubting him, just suggesting more assets to use.

Barton responds, "Oh, they will get their chance. Once we break through the first line of defense, at the gate, the law and military can follow behind us, arresting or killing anyone we may wound or miss. If we don't have to worry about what is going on behind us, then we can keep our eyes and guns moving forward. If everyone goes in, in a massive charge, all hell is going to break lose and someone is going to get killed, unnecessarily. If at all possible, I want to be in charge of the 'hell raising' and make sure it comes down on the right people."

Rand rubs his burly beard and blurts out, "If it were anyone else, Andy, I wouldn't give this plan a snowball's chance in hell. But you are just crazy enough to pull this off. And, apparently, we don't have much more sense than to follow you into the hornet's nest. As for a distraction, we have been sitting on a shipment of whiskey, vodka and other liquors that Livingston ordered a month ago. I can't see a bunch of stressed-up, crap-for brains barbarians turning down the 'nectar that settles your nerves'. What do you think?"

Barton thinks for a moment, then turns to Tomes, who gets a slight smile on his face and asks his cowboy friend an interesting question...

"You thinking what I am thinking? That, maybe, not only would they be willing to consider a shipment of booze, but they might just want to partake of a swig, or three, right there?"

Barton chuckles slightly, and then responds, "You can count on it. Let's hope so, because the only thing easier that shooting an idiot is shooting a drunk idiot."

With the deception plan in place, Barton turns to White Bear, "You have the hardest part in this thing. But I think you are up to it. After it gets dark, you have to find a way over the wall, enter the house, find Little Hawk, get both of you into a secure place and send a signal to us that we can start our push to get you out. All the time, being as invisible and discreet as you can be. Hopefully, a lot of the rich man's guns will be drawn to all the commotion that will be going on at the front gate. Make no mistake, use every trick to conceal your presence as you move around, because Livingston and Hartmann are not going to engage in the initial action. You think you can do it?"

White Bear looks at Swift Eagle, and says, "I am ready to do as you send me. I will die for the son of my chief, if that is what it takes."

Swift Eagle places his hand on the shoulder of his faithful

follower, and remarks, "You have been my friend since we were big enough to hold a bow and arrow, hunting game to feed the tribe. I should be the one to go, but Anderson is right in choosing you. I am injured and my mind is not clear enough to 'move like the panther on the snow' or be as silent as the night owl. The Great Spirits will go with you, you will be as uncatchable as the fog of morning."

Rand comes out from a backroom, in the cargo dock, holding a grappling hook and a long length of rope. Walking toward White Bear, he holds out the items for the Shawnee brave to take.

"Here, young man. You look wiry enough to shinny up this rope. I tore the sleeve off of an old shirt, wrapped it around the metal hook, so it wouldn't make as much noise when it catches on the limestone wall."

Tomes, shaking his head at the prospects of the plans, observes, "Well, that seems to take care of the 'distracting' and 'concealing" parts of your operation. I would say you, the chief and I will be involved in the 'shocking' portion of this little undertaking. I am sure you have this all thought out too, right!"

Barton, with no expression showing on his unshaven face, pulls his Henry rifle out of its sheath, jerks the cocking lever down and back, looks at Swift Eagle, and then, back at the waiting marshal.

"Our part is pretty simple, kill as many as we can, as fast as we can, and don't get killed. Nothing to it! If it moves, shoot it. If it is still moving, shoot it again. Keep moving forward and up, until we find Livingston. If he is the coward I think he is, he will be on the top floor, cowering behind something. Once he realizes he is alone, he will fold like an old tablecloth. If after the smoke clears he is still alive, then you can arrest him, shoot him, do whatever you feel like doing. Then, we find White Bear and Little Hawk and get out of Topeka. Let the marshals and the military clean up the mess and take the credit for bringing down the great Henry Livingston and his corrupt kingdom. I am not interested in watching them taking each other's pictures, maybe to be used for political aspirations someday."

Tomes laughs, flippantly, and asks, "You mean when your days as The Janitor are over, you wouldn't consider a career as an elected official of the great state of Kansas? Governor Anderson, I think it has the potential to put life in a political campaign, don't you think, Swift Eagle?"

The young Shawnee leader has no response, but Barton has a growing sneer across his face, and a low growl rolling in his throat, at the suggestion of the U.S. Marshal.

"Don't be a smart-ass, Tomes. You seem to have forgotten I back-handed you to the ground, one day, for talking to me in a foolish manner. First, you aren't ever going to let me out of being the Janitor because I do your dirty work for you. And second, you are the one who is always talking like one of those windbags in the government. While Swift Eagle and I will be hunting a twelve-point buck on the Rams Head River, you will be prancing around trying to impress the ladies at the Governor's Ball. So, just shut up, law dog!"

While Tomes stood with a dumbstruck look on his face, at his tall friend's reaction to his subtle attempt at humor, Barton turns away. As he walks past Swift Eagle and White Bear, he gives the surprised braves a reciprocation that seems to settle the mood...Barton winks.

With the main plans in place to get Little Hawk back, this unconventional band of allies spends the next couple of hours checking their guns, their horses and their fortitudes for the fight that is coming. Barton wishes that they could go and get it done now. But it will need to be nightfall for White Bear to have a chance of scaling the formidable wall and gaining entrance into the Livingston mansion. He is well aware that the somber hours of waiting can give them the chance to sharpen their minds and nerves for the challenge. Or they can let the ice in their veins be dissolved by the doubts that waiting can breed. Already, Barton hears the pleas of Rand encouraging Wilbur to stay strong and not worry. Although he doesn't understand much of the Shawnee language, the tall man is sure that Swift Eagle is offering the same positive prompting to his younger brave. Even Tomes, who is no stranger to daunting encounters, is observed to be showing signs of a foreboding sense of what awaits them. The marshal stares as his Colt pistol, occasional spinning the cartridge cylinder slowly, the clicking sound that it makes is almost hypnotic.

After a period of time, Barton steps outside of the cargo establishment. Not to get a breath of fresh air or to stretch his long legs, but to ascertain the root of a strange feeling that he has felt trying to manifest itself in his disposition. For over a year, Barton has, coldly and precisely, gone about executing his craft. 'Locate and eliminate' was his simple mantra, nothing more. But, this time, something was different. There felt like there was a veiled truth that he couldn't grasp, neither it's worth nor meaning. But, as he stood and stared at Jake, the buckskin horse, it finally came to his mind.

Smoke wasn't here. For the first time, and maybe the last time. Barton could always count on a simple talk, with the big gray horse, to provide a sense of validation of what he was about to do, and the outcome of it. Something as simple as running his hand over the mighty neck of his equine sidekick could be relaxing and therapeutic. Barton walked over to Jake and placed his hand on the side of the buckskin's shoulder. While the horse seemed to appreciate the attention, it just wasn't the same as Smoke.

"You are missing the big gray one, aren't you?" asked Tomes, walking outside where Barton was.

"Yeah, I almost whistled to call him here, but I remembered that wouldn't be happening today."

Tomes chuckled and replied, "Smoke does kind of grow on you. When you were laid up at Doc Tilley's, when Angus Ford shot you, I got to know Smoke a little better. Or maybe I should say he got to know me better. I think the big gray doesn't do anything unless it's his idea first."

Barton got a half-smile and shook his head, in the affirmative to Tomes' observation.

"You worried about tonight?" the marshal asks, changing the subject and the tone of their conversation.

Barton's eyebrows narrow and his lips tighten, as they often do when he is getting ready to speak a straight truth that might not be welcomed but is the truth anyway.

"Not really. Something has to be tried to get the kid. The plan is the only thing that we have to work with. Later tonight, that young Shawnee boy will be on his way back to his tribe, Livingston and a lot of his trash will be dead, and the state of Kansas will be glad to be rid of his corruption until someone else takes his place. I am pretty sure of all of that happening."

Tomes removes his hat, runs his fingers through his hair, and carefully probes Barton's thoughts, further.

"And, what part, if any, worries you, cowboy?"

Barton stops rubbing Jake, turns to Tomes, and responds, "Well, it really bothers me that you won't be paying attention, you get shot in the leg and won't be able to dance with the pretty girls at the Governor's Ball. Those fancy girls aren't going to be willing to be seen, on the dance floor with a gimpy lawman."

"You are about as funny as a drooling buzzard on a funeral hearse," Tomes grouses, as Barton smirks and walks back into the cargo facility.

"Alright, let's get loaded up and get riding. Don't forget why we are doing this, a scared little boy in the hands of some lowlife bastards."

After that proclamation, the preparations were finished. Barton, Tomes, Swift Eagle, White Bear, Rand, and Wilbur head toward the Livingston estate. The sun is setting upon the Kansas state capital, but the night is only beginning, and someone's life will end, soon.

15

"Hey, you clowns! This is not the greatest of times to be delivering furniture or garden tools to the Livingstons!"

That was the declaration that, loudly, came from the front gate of the walled residence. Seven armed guards step forward to greet Rand and Wilbur as they drive their cargo wagon up to the manor entrance.

Rand reaches behind him, pulls a weathered tarp off of a large wooden crate, and responds, "If we were hauling furniture or garden tools, I would agree with you, my friend. But, I have some of the finest drinking whiskey, Kentucky bourbon, and Russian vodka that any thirsty sentry might want to enjoy on a cool, Kansas night!"

The frowns that were meant to intimidate are replaced by the smiles of men who have not felt the smooth flow of good liquor sliding down their gullets in a long time. The hulking watchmen gather around the cargo wagon, grunts and growls of anticipation have replaced the barking and huffing of excoriation that greeted Rand and Wilber, upon their arrival.

"Open it up, cargo man," commanded the spokesman of the group, possessing a facial expression that could not be interpreted as anything other than ominous.

"Sorry, but I haven't been paid for this! Until I have the money, or a promissory note, in my hand, I am afraid the unofficial party is on hold," was Rand's response.

The captain of the guards inspects the crate closer. Taking the butt of his rifle, he pokes and punches at the wooden container, as if he could make it break open, for all to admire and behold.

"Surely, it wouldn't cost anything for a man to size up what manner of wares that you are bringing to us tonight," the large, formidable man asks, faking a sense of niceness as he appeals to the unbending Rand.

"Sorry, no looks, no touches, no tastes! Nothing until I see coin, cash or gold nugget in my hand, and that is the way it is," was Rand's uneasy reply.

Then, another rugged voice from the group of guards speaks up, "Hey Gus, wasn't it these two shippers that helped that nosey cowboy get into the house? Remember, the boss had the hell beat out of him and carted out to the edge of town. I am sure it was these two haulers!"

Suddenly, the pseudo look of niceness leaves Gus' face and is replaced by an expression of disdain. The large man looks over Rand, then moves to the back of the wagon to scrutinize Wilbur, who is now sweating and trembling uncontrollably.

"Are you trying to pull one over on us, cargo man?" the large sentry barks.

"No, I told you that I have a load of liquor for Livingston. And, as soon as I speak to someone with the authority to sign off on the bill, I will be more than happy to let you look, touch, and drink all of it you want," answered Rand, concerned with the changing tone of this preliminary encounter.

Gus steps back from the wagon, cocks the lever on his Winchester rifle, and proclaims, "If you aren't hiding anything in the box, then you won't mind if I do this!"

Bang...Bang...Bang...Bang!

The sound of gunfire, glass breaking, and wood splintering rises through the Kansas evening, as Gus fires his weapon into the cargo box. The result of the armed assault was various streams of golden liquid trickling out of the cracks, and bullet holes, of the pine-board container. As he leaps forward to stop any more carnage to his valuable cargo, Rand is met by Gus thrusting the butt of his long gun into the abdomen of the burly shipper...

"Aargh" was Rand's pained groan as he crumpled to the ground.

"Let's whoop it up," was bellowed as more sentries jumped up on the wagon to grab their shares of the spiritous treasure. Wilbur was no deterrent to the onslaught as his protests were met by a pistol to the side of his face, causing him to fall off of the buckboard transport.

Gathered in a grove of cherry trees across the property, unnoticed by the band of revelers, are Barton, Tomes, and Swift Eagle. Barton stands to his feet. He raises his Henry rifle to his shoulder, pulls the cocking lever down and back to its original position, and starts to squeeze the trigger, intending to fire across at those that had attacked Rand and Wilbur.

"Wait, just wait," was the plea of Marshal Tomes! "You shoot now, and White Bear will never be able to get into the manor and find Little Hawk. Look! Look at the front door of the house! Wait just a minute, it's working!"

When he lowered his rifle and watched where the lawman had directed, Barton noticed that more guards were emerging out of the Livingston mansion, drawn by the sound of gunfire. It did not take long for them to join in the impromptu celebration that was going on at the front gate. Barton counted, at least, eight additional lookouts joining their rowdy cronies. Chances were there were fewer Livingston men in the back of the building, thus lowering the odds of White Bear being confronted, once he made it over the wall and into the mansion.

Tomes, continuing to watch the carousing band of thugs, says, "I know it's hard to watch and wait, but Rand and Wilbur will be ok. I hope that the big guard didn't shoot up all of the booze. Let's permit them to drink for a bit. For now, their minds are on blowing off some steam and tension, and that will play into our hands. If they get a little sloshed, that can only make our part easier when White Bear gives us the signal that he and the boy are safe. Remember what I told you once, never get in a hurry to get shot or killed."

Barton lowers the Henry rifle, leans back against a young fruit tree, and replies, "We will wait."

It was around twenty minutes after the boozing had started that the revelers started showing signs that the liquor was doing its part of the plan. Slurred words, bickering, and staggering gave the impression that the rowdy guards were not at the top of their vocations. Laughing, cursing and back-slapping added to the impression that the time was getting right for the third part of Barton's plan, the 'shock' of an all-out assault upon the estate. All they needed was a signal from White Bear, that he and Little Hawk were secure. And then, suddenly, a cry comes from within the Livingston manor...

"Fire! Fire on the third floor!"

As black, thick smoke billows from an upper window toward the back of the mansion, Tomes turns to Barton and calmly asks, "Do you reckon that could be a signal?"

Barton, without any wavering in his resolute expression or tone, replies, "Works for me!"

The three men start running toward the front entrance gates, the drunken guards having no idea of the hell that is about to be unleashed upon them. As had been discussed in an earlier strategy discussion, Swift Eagle stops and pulls four arrows out of his quiver. Calmly, he places each one upon the string of his hunting bow, and pulls and releases four times. Within seconds, they are sailing through the night air, in search of their inebriated targets. Summarily, four sentries go down, never knowing what the source of their unforeseen demise was. The other drunken brutes laugh, thinking that their fellow partiers cannot hold their liquor and are just taking a break from the abundant frivolities.

"Here, this will serve you better from this point on," Barton yells to Swift Eagle, as he tosses the young Shawnee brave his Henry rifle.

Once the initial shooting starts, it will be over within ten minutes or so. Barton, Tomes, and Swift Eagle take cover behind Rand's cargo wagon, the smell of expensive alcohol still hanging in the air. Although still in varied stages of drunkenness, the guards realize that they are under attack and muster enough cognizance to attempt to return fire. But the 'distraction and shock' aspects of the extrication plan have been successful. When the smoke clears, a few of Livingston's thugs will be standing with their hands in the air, deciding that surrender is better than sacrifice. But many will not fight again, this day or any day.

Once they have checked on Rand and Wilbur and are assured that each is alright, the trio of rescuers moves forward to the front door of the large house, reloading and preparing to enter inside once there. Behind the three, a group of marshals and soldiers move into position at the front gate, posed to take care of any remaining obstacles or problems left behind by Barton, Tomes, and Swift Eagle.

"It's going to get harder from here," Barton says, as he reloads his Colt revolver. "They know we are coming, now. You two stay to the right, I will move from the left. Once Tomes and I get to the top of a staircase, Swift Eagle will follow as we keep watch. Keep moving together, no one breaks off by themselves. If anyone empties their gun, then we wait until we are all loaded and ready to resume. If you start running out of ammo, take available shells off of the nearest dead body you can find. Should you get shot, find the nearest cover and wait for the trailing marshals and soldiers to find you. Any questions, gentlemen?"

Barton looks at Tomes and Swift Eagle and sees that the two men are ready to get this thing finished. As he starts to step inside the front door, the thought crosses his mind that if this is a cause to die for, he could do worse than to have the company of the marshal and the young Shawnee chief along on this endeavor.

"Let's hit em' hard, gentlemen!"

Methodically, and with the precision of a surgeon, the three-some work their way up the stairs and down the halls of each floor. While resistance is not heavy, due to the large number of gunmen neutralized at the front gate, it is ever-present. As Barton and Tomes check inside the rooms on the side of the passage that they are working down, Swift Eagle watches ahead for approaching assailants. Tomes is amazed at how coldly, and matter-of-factly, his friend confronts and remedies each gunman he makes contact with. While Barton is not the same man Tomes first met and rode with years ago, the lawman still has that same comfort of knowing that Barton is nearby.

Once they have gone through the first two floors and cleared out any Livingston heavies taking positions there, or discovered house staff hiding from the gunfire, there is only one more place to clear out, the third floor. Barton is certain that White Bear and Little Hawk are somewhere on that level. And he is certain that Livingston can be found hiding there. He is not surprised that Hartmann hasn't shown his face, or gun, in the initial battles. Barton got the feeling, when they ran into each other at the stone wall where Smoke was hit by a Livingston hireling's bullet, that the arrogant gunman was all talk. But things are different now. Before, Hartmann was acting out of greed for a reward. Now, it will be about Hartmann's very survival from Barton's retribution for what happened that day.

Suddenly, as they work their way up toward the top of the last staircase, a shot rings out.

"Damn it, to hell," cries out Tomes, in evident pain.

"You hit bad?" Barton inquires?

"No, I am more pissed than hurt. I should have seen that one coming. Looked down for a minute and someone got a lucky shot off. Damn it, to hell!"

Barton calls over to Swift Eagle, "Hey Chief, how is he looking?'

The young Shawnee bravely leans over and examines the wound in Tomes' thigh, and with a straight face responds, "Anderson, I don't think he will be dancing with those squaws that you talked about at the white man's gathering."

Barton, unexpectedly, chuckles at the attempt at humor by Swift Eagle.

Barton retorts, "Maybe we should just put him out of his misery, what do you say?"

Tomes, irritably, shouts back, "Oh, shut up, you smart ass!"

Bang...Bang...Bang...Bang!

More gunfire erupts from the top of the remaining staircase to be navigated. After reloading his sidearm, one more time,

Barton yells, "Come on, Swift Eagle! Take Tomes' place and let's get this done!"

Before the young chief can step over the wounded lawman, Tomes lifts himself up and announces, "You aren't going anywhere without me, cowboy. You take care of your side, and we will batten down things over here."

With their guns blazing, the trio make their way to the top of the third staircase, putting down two more of Livingston's hired men. Once the echoes of gunfire die down, in the oaken hallway, tense voices can be heard arguing in a distant room. It doesn't take long to discern that the two bickering mouths belong to Livingston and Hartmann. It seems that Livingston is screaming for Hartmann to go out into the hallway and kill the advancing intruders. Hartmann's response was in the line of 'getting paid a lot more' to do it. Barton smirked as he realized that his assessment of Hartmann as a 'chicken-crap loudmouth' was true.

Tomes asks, "Do you think that they are the only ones left? Livingston sounds kind of desperate and out of options."

Barton thinks for a minute, then turns to Swift Eagle, and says, "I remember hearing something the night that Seth, Smoke, and I were stranded at that place where we were ambushed by Hartmann. I thought it was birds chirping and singing. But later I realized that it was White Bear and the other braves communicating with each other. Is there some way for you to relay to White Bear that we are here and for him to disclose where he is, without Livingston finding out?"

Swift Eagle places his hands together and brings them to his mouth. The young Shawnee chief makes a couple of sounds reminiscent of the Kansas screech owl. He waits, gets no response, and tries again. Barton notices that with each attempt, Swift Eagle gets a deeper look of concern on his face.

"He should be giving you some response, shouldn't h?,"

quizzes Barton. Tomes, troubled by the silence, waits for an answer too.

Swift Eagle replies, "White Bear may have found Little Hawk, but they are not safe now. My call was a sign that we are close, and he can respond. He has not returned my hail because he is dead, injured or Little Hawk is being threatened if he does."

Tomes, concerned now for both lives, asks, "Barton, do you think Livingston has them?"

Before he can answer, Hartmann's voice comes roaring out of what is the family parlor, at the end of the third-floor hallway.

"Hey, bounty hunter, I have the Indian kid! He is crying and saying something in that native gibberish they use. You come any closer and I will put a bullet through his little head. I ain't going to miss from point-blank range. Oh, and don't plan on that bigger wahoo helping him. That red trash is a little busy bleeding all over the boss' rug. Seems he didn't have any 'wampum magic' that would hide him from a .45 slug heading his way. It's up to you, bounty hunter! Are we going to continue to make noise or are we going to play nice?"

As Swift Eagle stands and stares at where the voice is coming from, and where he knows his son is being held, Tomes steps across the hall to where Barton is, calmly, reloading his Colt pistol.

"I would imagine that, while you were coming up with the initial plan to get Little Hawk out of here, you devised another plan in case the first one didn't work, right?"

Barton, not looking up from his re-loading, unshakably answers, "Who says the first one is not still working?"

Tomes shakes his head. Surprised by his friend's answer, the federal lawman pushes for an explanation.

"I'm sorry! Nowhere in your summary of how we were going to pull this off, do I remember the part where Livingston and

Hartmann are holding up in a large room, Little Hawk has a rather powerful gun pointed at him and White Bear is of no use because he has been shot. Was I not there when you covered that part?"

Barton points his handgun up, pulls the hammer back, gives the cartridge chamber a spin, slowly releases the hammer, and looks at the marshal with a look that could stop the hands of an expensive Swiss clock.

"From the beginning, the plan has been to kill Hartmann and Livingston, get the boy, and go home. I don't see that happening while we stand here whining about the situation. I say we finish what we came here for."

Barton takes a few steps toward the end of the hallway, making sure that his cowboy boots make enough noise for Livingston and Hartmann to know that he is closer to them. He knows that the next gains he makes, in this standoff, may start with testing the nerves and resolve of his opponents, rather than whose guns are bigger or faster. After letting the quiet of the moment wear on the men holding up in the family room, Barton takes a few more steps, cocks his Colt, and waits for a response to come trumpeting from the end of the hall.

"Don't be stupid, trail trash!" Livingston yells out. "Hartmann is not lying. He has the Indian kid, and he isn't being gentle with him. If you think you are the only one that can kill people and not care, I don't think Hartmann is going to lose any sleep over ridding the world of another insignificant redskin. Do you hear me, trail trash?"

Barton senses that the situation will not stand much more stress, that a cornered animal will lash out eventually. Barton waves for Tomes and Swift Eagle to work their way up to him. Once the three men are assembled, Barton leads them to just outside the parlor entrance, but stays out of sight of the stressed combatants inside.

"Ok, Livingston, what is it going to take to get the boy and the bleeding brave out of there? Here is an idea for you to chew on. You give us the boy, the wounded warrior, and the right to put a bullet in Hartmann, and we will consider getting you a deal with the U.S. marshals. Maybe get them to put you up in one of those cushy prisons that rich people go to. What do you think, big shot?"

Tomes grabs Barton's arm and gives him a hard stare that says that they don't have the right to make any deal like that. Barton just raises his hand and responds with his own facial expression, one to encourage the lawman to have patience with Barton's thinking and tactics.

"Who do you think you are?" Livingston angrily responds. "You have nothing to negotiate with! We have the boy and the brave, we hold all the cards. You don't want to get this kid killed. And that is what is going to happen if you don't take your associates and get out of my house. You get out of here, and take all those marshals and soldiers with you. All of you will get off of my property. If I see a gun, a badge, or a military uniform when I look out this window, thirty minutes from now, I will start killing me some redskins. Do you hear me, gunslinger?"

"You are assuming that I care about your hostages, money bags," Barton unpretentiously answers. "What if I don't give a damn about them and I am just here for the reward that has been put up for you and your hired slacker. I was told the money would be good 'dead or alive'. Nobody mentioned any set number of casualties that would entail."

"You're crazy, trail trash! You wouldn't go to all the trouble and risk of coming up here if you didn't care. You aren't fooling anyone. Get out now or I am going to have the kid killed. Do you hear me?"

Before Barton can respond, another voice enters into the discourse...

"He won't kill the child, I will not let him."

Barton, Tomes, and Swift Eagle are stunned when they turn to see who else is on the third floor with them, now placing themselves into the mix of this complex confrontation.

It is Hannah Livingston, Henry Livingston's wife.

16

"Mam, I think you should go downstairs and get out of here, before you get hurt!"

Barton waits as Tomes pleads with the well-dressed women. She seems to be oblivious to the marshal's frantic appeals, almost like she is in a trance or state of shock. Seeing that she was not going to remove herself from the danger of the moment, Barton turns to Tomes with an unexpected proposition.

"Let her give it a try."

The U.S. marshal reacts in the way a lawman normally would, especially when he is thinking of the procedures and rules of not letting innocent bystanders get involved, or in the way, of an active confrontation.

"Have you lost your mind, Barton? We send her in there, then he has three hostages to use against us."

Barton studies Ms. Livingston, who is displaying the look of a woman who is watching her whole world fall down around her. After a few moments of rolling a growing idea around in his head, Barton responds to the marshal's honest concern for the welfare of the lady of the manor.

"I am not thinking that we, actually, send her in there. But, let her stand here in the doorway of the parlor room. Maybe, just seeing her could shake something up in that thick head of his. Let her speak to him from here, we will stand on each side of her. We can be out of sight, but ready to step in if anything seems to be going wrong. It may not be the greatest move that we could make, but I don't see that we have anything else."

Tomes is slow to agree to his friend's precarious idea. But he knows that time is not their ally and there is a rising truth in Barton's impression that they don't have any other workable options for rescuing Little Hawk and White Bear. A few more moments of reflection leads Tomes to turn to Ms. Livingston and establish some rules for her engagement with her husband.

"Mam, if we are going to do this thing, then you have to do as you are told. Your husband is desperate and realizes he has nothing to lose at this point. You stand in the entrance to the sitting room, you say your peace and then you move back, out of the way. You don't go in, you don't make any offers to help him, you don't negotiate with him. You just try to get him to do the right thing and let the child go. Do you agree?"

The solemn woman, slowly, shakes her head to the affirmative and takes her place where she can be seen by all who are in the large, dimly-lit chamber. Barton, Tomes, and Swift Eagle move as close as they can, without being seen. Upon the encouragement of the lawman, the earnest wife begins her intercession.

"Henry, this has got to stop! Please, let the child come to me before this goes any further. I have turned my eyes away from the unscrupulous ways you have conducted your businesses. I have even ignored the lives you have ruined in your pursuit of power and finances. But there are people lying dead in our house, and the smell of gun smoke hangs in every hallway. And, for what? Necessary sacrifices to sustain the 'Livingston lifestyle'? No more, Henry. I will not let a child be used as nothing more than a chess piece in some doomed game you are playing."

Livingston, after the sight of his pleading wife provokes his mind to race, shakes his head and snaps, "Hannah, get out of here! I did all of this for you and now look what it's got me! Woman, go back to the cathouse I found you in. I wouldn't be in this mess if it hadn't been for you wanting a damn kid of your own. I am going to kill that black bastard that took the kid, he is responsible for all of this. He had no right to take the kid back to the rancher, no right at all!"

Hesitating a moment, Ms. Livingston delivers a startling bit of information that will be like touching a burning match to a box of gunpowder.

"Jeremiah wasn't acting independently when he took Jackson from school, that day. He was just doing what he was told. You see, I instructed Jeremiah to find Mr. Anderson and take Jackson to him. I couldn't live with the fact that you had bought a child that had been taken from his father. Yes, I wanted a child, but not that way. So, I am the one who sent Jackson back to his rightful place. And I gave Jeremiah money to leave Topeka because I knew you would get angry and have him hurt, just like you did the man who came looking for his son. No more hurting, no more killing, this all stops now!"

Livingston is now reeling, emotionally and mentally, as he tries to process this staggering revelation. He looks at his wife, looks at the derringer pistol that he is holding in his hand, looks back up at the crying woman standing before him, and then screams...

"You back-stabbing whore!"

Bang!

The rich man's wife is, instantly, knocked backward as the .32

caliber bullet impacts her shoulder and enters her body. With instincts sharpened during his exploits as the 'janitor', Barton steps out from where he has been standing, and catches the stumbling Hannah with his left arm. Simultaneously, in an equally adept move with his right hand, he clears his Colt of its holster and gets off two shots.

Bang...Bang!

So lightning quick and effortless was Barton's counteraction that neither intended target sees it coming or has a chance. In less than two seconds, Barton has put a .45 caliber hole in Livingston's greedy heart and placed the other between Hartmann's eyes. The Colt slug would be the last thing to ever pass thru the hired gunman's heinous mind. Hartmann's grip on Little Hawk is broken as his life, expeditiously, ebbs from him. The Shawnee youngster runs to Swift Eagle, who embraces his released son and gives Barton a handwave of gratefulness. Barton, true to form, returns the chief's gesture of gratitude with a half-smile and a nod of the head.

Tomes rushes into the room, smoke still hanging in the air from Barton's quick action that brings the impassioned encounter to a close. The marshal thumps Livingston's lifeless body with his boot, moves to the nearby Hartmann, and gets the same response from the face-down gunslinger. Satisfied with the results of his examination, Tomes looks up at Barton and says the only thing that would be appropriate at the moment.

"Good enough, cowboy!"

Lawmen and military people will come in, and out, of the parlor room for the next hour. A couple of army medics will treat the wounds of Hannah Livingston and White Bear, which are deemed serious, but not life-threatening. Barton was not surprised that the young Shawnee brave's wound was in the back, further cementing his opinion of Hartmann as a cheap-shot artist. Tomes will explain, to his federal superiors, how the events unfolded. He will tell of how high the threat level was for the innocents in the room, that there was no other action that could be taken and not lose those innocent lives. And, to make sure that all legal aspects are covered, and no questions are raised, Tomes explains how Barton acted as a sworn officer of the government, taking his oath to the Marshal's Service before they started their mission of rescue. It was this last part of Tomes' presentation that caused Barton to walk away, slowly shaking his head and rolling his eyes, amazed at how his lawman friend was still having to cover for him.

As Barton heads out of the parlor room, he walks past Ms. Livingston, still being treated by the army medical officer. He stops for a moment, then makes a rather honest assessment of her wound and her former life.

"You are lucky your husband was as piss-poor a shooter as he was as a husband."

The newly widowed woman tries to smile at the tall man's straight-forward statement, her shoulder burning with pain as the medic treats it with alcohol and another antiseptic medicine.

"I am so sorry, Mr. Anderson, I truly am. I did not know the truth about Jackson, or should I say Seth. I did not know what unscrupulous measures that my husband had taken to arrange for us to have a child. I did not know until that day when you came here, looking for your son. Over the years, I have turned my head to a lot of the dishonest things Henry did, in the name of doing business. But, what he did to you, simply because you loved your son and wanted him back, that was a line that I could not cross. I know you may not accept it, but I offer my regrets from the deepest part of my heart, I truly do."

Barton takes a moment to let what has been said to sink in, trying not to let the swirling emotions of the moment cloud his mind. After a few more seconds of reflection have passed by, he gives her the most sincere acknowledgment that he will ever give anyone...he reaches up and tips his hat toward her.

Before he can walk away, Barton is halted by the next words that Ms. Livingston speaks, her voice starting to quiver and exhibit signs of a new reality sinking in.

"I loved your son, Mr. Anderson, I truly did. I loved him like no other before. He was such a light in my life, as you can imagine after experiencing the 'Livingston way'. He is a good boy, a kind and tender boy. That was why I could not allow him to be here anymore. I am sorry about what happened to your family. I wish I could have met Seth's mother. You and she did a great job with Seth. I am sorry, for I seem to be rambling. I just can't believe it's all over. I just wish, I just wish..."

Barton watches as this broken lady fights to hold her composure. As he scrutinizes her, as she continues to look up at him, he senses that this conversation is not yet finished.

"There is something you wish to say or ask?"

The tears are now flowing more freely. After taking a big breath, the wishful lady responds.

"I have no right to ask, and you have every right to say no. I understand that. But do you think it would be possible when enough time has passed, that I could send a birthday card or Christmas card to Seth? My heart is not going to completely forget him, even if he is no longer a part of my life. Maybe, someday, I could come and visit him? That is, if it is alright with you, and of course, with Seth?"

Barton says nothing, his face not showing a sign of any position that he is taking on the sincere requests that have been made. He leans over, picks up his Henry rifle that Swift Eagle had leaned against a large end table, and makes a move in the direction of the exit from the sitting lounge. Abruptly, he stops and turns back to the awaiting woman, tears are still streaming down her hopeful face.

"The second day of December. Smithview, Kansas. Let's start with a birthday card and see how it goes from there."

And, with that word of glimmering possibility, Barton turns and leaves behind any toll that his exposure to the 'world of Henry Livingston' has taken from him, and Seth.

Later on, outside the mansion, the scene of the initial gunbattle will be put in order. Bodies are placed on wagons and carts to be transported away from the front gate. Shell casings are picked up and placed in a pillowcase, to be taken and reloaded by the budget-restrained army. Rand and Wilbur, having had their bruises and abrasions looked after by a military medic, prepare to take their team and rig back to their shipping warehouse. Barton, Tomes, and Swift Eagle have rounded up their horses, from the cherry grove, and are riding back toward the cargo men. White Bear, although not in the best shape for the long return to the tribe, is with them.

"Gentlemen, I don't know what we would have done without your help," Tomes begins. "I am sure that there have to be some wanted posters on some of the Livingston men that were killed today. When I get to a place where I can tie up all the loose ends, I will make sure any monies owed reach the appropriate parties. Until then, I can say it's been an honor to work with each of you, the state of Kansas thanks you, and the U.S. government thanks you."

Barton pulls up beside the marshal and shares that if there are any bounties, on any Livingston men, just give his portion to the Shawnee people to help replace some of the things that were taken, or destroyed, when Hartmann's gang raided their tribal camp. Tomes, taking on the demeanor of one who is about to give his friend some bad news, informs Barton that he will not be receiving any of the reward monies. When Barton responds with a facial expression that commands an explanation, the U.S. marshal reciprocates.

"You see when I reported that you entered into the confrontation as a 'temporarily sworn-in deputy marshal', that meant that you were disqualified from any financial gains or rewards because you were a representative of the federal government. So, I had already planned to give your part to Swift Eagle's people and to Rand. It seems that you have never returned the Morgan horse that he loaned you. Plus, there is the cost of the liquor that was shot up. Sorry, cowboy, but we will just strike this one up as 'doing it out of the goodness of your big ol' heart.'"

"Oh, aren't you just one to always do the right thing," snapped Barton, as Tomes chuckled at him.

With the handshakes and farewells concluded, the four men mount up and prepare to leave Topeka, together. Or, at least, that is what Barton is thinking until his accounting of the travel party is revised by the one who is wearing the federal badge on his chest.

"Well, gentlemen! It has not been boring, that is for sure. And it is always a pleasure when you can leave a town with as many souls as you entered it with. Oh, that's right, we gained one. And that makes it even better to have Little Hawk with us. But this is where I must leave you, I have pressing business in Prestonburg and am expected to be there by tomorrow night."

Barton is curious as to the nature of the matters that seem to have occupied the marshal's consideration. After pulling Jake closer to Hickory, Barton starts his inquisition into the travel plans of the departing marshal.

"Exactly what have you gotten yourself involved in, lawman? Some sort of range war? Or maybe a crime spree has broken out in Prestonburg and there is only one federal badge that is up to the task of returning order. What is it, Marshal Tomes?"

When the marshal is hesitant to answer, this just intrigues Barton the more. Not willing to let it go, he continues to offer possible objectives that would call for his law friend to have to make haste in arriving in Prestonburg. After the growing line of rationales starts to exasperate him, Tomes blurts out the surprising motivation for him to leave this band of travelers.

"If you must know, and minding your own business is not an option for that thick head of yours, I have to be in Prestonburg tomorrow night because I am to have a dinner appointment!"

Barton is stunned at this surprising revelation but is not satisfied to just leave it there. The fact that he sees that it is making Tomes uncomfortable, to elaborate any further, is just like 'waving a red handkerchief in the face of an enraged bull'. So, Barton continues to press on.

"You have an actual living, breathing female that wants to spend time with you. What is her problem? Is she blind? Is she, how do I say this, not exactly what you would call a handsome woman? Come on, Tomes. Why is this woman so desperate that she finds you as adequate dinner company?"

Tomes is now at the end of his patience and announces, "If you must know, I have the honor of sharing the company of an attractive lady who, not so long ago, helped save your life!"

Barton thinks for a second and then responds, "Oh, no! Oh, hell no! Not Nurse Baird! She is a fine lady, an attractive woman who can surely do better than an old law dog like you! What are you holding over her to cause her to endure such a hellacious encounter?"

Tomes, now, realizes that his tall friend is having too much fun with this exaggerated line of questioning. So, he decides to 'turn the tables' on his interrogator and not respond, knowing that the sudden stoppage of information will cause Barton to get agitated by the silence. After holding back any further revelations on the subject, Tomes smiles and resumes sharing what he thinks his friend deserves to know.

"Wanda and I have been seeing each other, on the occasions that I am in the area. When she is not needed at the clinic, we visit or go out for something to eat. That's about it. Just two friends sharing a meal, a laugh, or a shoulder if the situation calls for it. And, for your information, she doesn't see me as a broken-down law officer. I think she likes my company as much as I appreciate hers."

"Oh, she is Wanda now? To the rest of the world, she is Nurse Baird, but you are so special that you get to call her Wanda. Marshal, you have definitely done better than anyone would have imagined."

Tomes tugs on Hickory's reins, causing him to pull away from the traveling band of riders. Speaking back over his shoulder, the marshal comments, "Cowboy, I won't argue with you on that point. She is a lot better than I deserve, that's for sure. But I am going to do right by this opportunity for as long as she will put up with me. Who knows where this might lead?"

Barton smirks as he puts the heels of his boots into Jake's sides and answers," Don't push your luck, lawman. She may not be blind, but I am sure she is not desperate, either."

And with that parting jab, the unusual grouping of personalities go their separate ways. Soon, Tomes will be out of sight as he proceeds to Prestonburg. The remainder of the riding configuration will be headed to the Shawnee camp, where the tribe awaits their new chief and the future leader of the people of the High Plains Shawnee nation.

17

The autumn sun is rising on another brisk Kansas morning. Barton figures it will take them almost two days to return to Swift Eagles' tribe, on the northern part of Asa Givens' ranch. With White Bear recovering from a bullet wound and the care of a young child, this journey cannot, and will not, be rushed. Barton finds it reminds him of the situation that he was in, not so long ago. He was still recovering from the injuries caused by the Livingston men. Seth, although a little older than Little Hawk, had to be considered in the most careful ways, too.

The mood of the riders is optimistic. A few hours of rest, a warm campfire, and the preparation of a basic breakfast has positioned them to continue their journey under hopeful conditions. As had been the case, for most of the trip, the three Shawnee males conversed among themselves. While not versed in the Shawnee dialect, Barton would recognize an occasional word or term. When added to the tone of the conversations, and the facial expressions that accompanied the discussions, Barton felt like Swift Eagle was explaining, to Little Hawk, what to expect when they got back to the Indian encampment. Again, he can relate to the chore that Swift Eagle was dealing with, as Barton had the same heart-wrenching experience with Seth. Barton thought on the valid fact that, even though they came from diverse cultures, people have a way of navigating the same life conditions and experiences.

Barton, not one for lengthy conversations or in-depth discussions, didn't feel that he was being ignored. The fact is, he will not be a part of any long-term plans when it comes to the High Plains Shawnee nation. Once they get to their destination, Barton will be sensitive to the traditions of Swift Eagle's people, their need to celebrate the return of their young chief, and the victory of getting Little Hawk back. Swift Eagle had explained that his people had had everything taken from them, by the white man's government. Everything, except for their memories and their fireside talks of 'Shadow Warriors', 'Wind Runners' and someday walking with the great Spirits of their historical clans. It will be of profound importance for the Shawnee tribesmen to welcome 'Judeahay' to sit at their campfire, smoke the tribal pipe, and re-tell stories of how the evil men were defeated. Usually, the more the pipe is smoked, the bigger the stories get. His participation will help return a sense of dignity, pride, and honor to a people who have been at the mercy of others' wishes and demands for a long time. Barton figures if he can take bad men's lives, he should volunteer to play a part in good people having a life again. He thought of how good it was going to be when he, Seth, and Smoke were all united again, around their campfire, telling their stories of how good life would be.

It was about two hours after they had resumed their travel that Swift Eagle turned to Barton and asked a question that seemed out of the norm of what was transpiring, so far.

"Anderson, are you expecting that we should be joining up with someone?"

Barton looks in the direction that the young Shawnee chief is observing and notices four riders heading in their direction. As they get closer, he studies the unexpected strangers, never one to take anything for granted or as just happenstance. The pace with which they are riding does not present them as a threat, yet. The road that they are riding on is often traveled, especially when going from Topeka to Smithview. So, just a chance meeting, perhaps? Barton is not in a line of work that allows for chance to be an influencing factor, and this encounter will not be an exception to his unbending rule of survival.

It didn't take long for Barton's sense of concern to be raised to a status of high alert. The first thing that he notices is that the men are rough, in appearance and conduct. The approaching riders have a penchant for talking loudly and pointing, mostly in the direction of his Indian co-riders. Barton's hope that they will just ride on and not engage in any form of exchange is quickly dashed. Upon reaching the approaching drifters, one raises his voice above the chatter of the other riders.

"Hey look, boys! I think we have just rode up on a great Indian warrior. I'll be if it's not ol' Chief Sitting Bull, himself!"

The other riders laugh and point in Swift Eagle's direction. The young Indian sovereign does not give them the pleasure of his attention, but he just keeps looking in the forward direction.

"No, wait! I am mistaken. It's not ol' Sitting Bull, but I think it's his long lost, bastard kid, Full of Bull," continues the obnoxious taunts of the louder of the four strangers. Barton notices that one of the men is not finding any humor in his large friend's barbs, but just sits and watches for a reaction from the tall man on the buckskin horse. For now, Barton will just keep riding, his right hand working its way toward the holster that holds his .45 Colt revolver.

"Hey, I am talking to you, red dogs! Don't just ride away and act like I am not worth greeting. You think you are too good for us, you redskin vermin!"

It is at this point, that Barton pulls back on the reins of Jake, puts his left boot heel into the side of the big horse, and spins around. With a cold, impassive look on his face, Barton sits and waits for the next barrage of ignorance to come out of the large ruffian's mouth.

"Let us go, Anderson," Swift Eagle pleads. "It is nothing that we have not heard before and will hear again. Let us continue to travel back to my people, who await the arrival of their chief and the Shadow Warrior!"

While he wishes that it could be so easy, Barton knows that these curs are not through with their show of witless bravado. It is not long before his expectations are confirmed, as the interlopers swing around and are now facing Barton. Three of the roughnecks continue to point and throw verbal aggression upon the Shawnee braves, the fourth man persists in his stare at Barton. When Barton instructs Swift Eagle to move Little Hawk out of the line of the confrontation, the larger of the thugs resumes his verbal line of insults.

"You see that, Frank! Just as I thought, the redskins are going to hide behind the white man's gun. You willing to die for those red dogs, Indian lover?"

Barton continues to say nothing, just waits to see who will make the first move, who will tip off where this ends up, or who will have the sense to get their loudmouth compadre under control. Just when it seems that a violent confrontation cannot be avoided, the silent one speaks.

"Eh, Wayne, you might want to shut up and consider who you are pissing off here. I might suggest you give it a rest and just ride away, while you can."

The bigmouth glances at his concerned friend, looks back at

Barton, then guffaws, and continues with his display of unin-formed arrogance.

"Well now, Frank! Who do you think this Indian lover is? Who am I supposed to be so terrified of? Is he Wild Bill Hickok? No, I know who he is. With that big Henry rifle in his saddle sheath, it's none other than Buffalo Bill Cody. That's who it is, isn't it, Frank?"

Barton gives the braggart no attention, but continues to share eye-to-eye contact with the one who may have enough sense to move this explosive moment into a less volatile incident.

"No, Wayne. It's not Hickok or Cody. I would be more sure if he was sitting upon a dark gray horse. But the Henry gives me pause as to who we are stationed in front of. You are him, aren't you, big man?"

Barton says nothing, just sits resolutely upon Jake. While he would rather be astride Smoke, Barton is impressed that the buckskin seems aware of the seriousness of the moment and is steadfast in his support of his rider.

"Enough, Frank! Who the hell do you think this great Indian protector is?" bellows the brawny blowhard.

"Wayne, you are insulting that crazy Smithview rancher who killed Angus Ford, Coy Newton and a slew of other outlaws who were a lot better with a gun than you are!"

Suddenly, the one who has been the spokesman for the group swallows deeply, takes a more somber tone of voice, and asks, "Are you that obsessed, murdering son-of-a-bitch?"

Barton, cooly, responds, "That's Mr. Son-of-a-Bitch, to you."

As the four strangers have a discussion amongst themselves, hopefully on how to save face and ride away, Barton looks behind him to check on his native friends. Swift Eagle has Little Hawk sitting behind him and has his pony positioned in front of White Bear. Barton is impressed by the young Shawnee chief's willingness to put himself in danger to protect those who are under his leadership.

Upon turning back to the matters before him, a humbled Wayne seems to be ready to negotiate a satisfactory ending to this unfortunate encounter.

"Well, it must be your lucky day, gunslinger! I have talked it over with my partners, and we have come to an agreement that we are going to let you, and your redskin friends, ride on. I would rather just kill you and let the coyotes have you. But my friends don't have quite the backbone I have. So, turn tail and run on, before I change my mind, Mr. Son-of-a-Bitch!"

If it had just been Barton sitting here, this day, he might have been willing to see how much the bigmouth was willing to back up. But the objective of this whole journey has been to get Little Hawk back to his people, and for Barton to get Smoke and Seth on the trail to Smithview. So, with a nudge of a boot heel, Jake turns around and heads to rejoin the original travel party. And it seemed like disaster had been avoided, until...

"Hey, saddle tramp, turn your coward ass back around and face me!"

The demand, unmistakably, is called out from the one named Wayne. When Barton gets Jake turned around, he is surprised to see the brawny stranger is sitting alone, the other three are sitting off to the side. Riding up to where he is closer to the confrontation, Barton says six words, hoping that they might give this one another chance to ride away.

"You don't have to do this."

Wayne pulls his coat back, freeing his ability to access his .44 Army revolver with an eight-inch barrel. With his lips drawn tight, and his face wrinkled under the stress of the moment, the brawny man offers the best explanation he can for why this was going to happen.

"You see, I do have to. They are my friends, they look up to me. You embarrassed me in front of them. I can't ride with them, with this ending any other way. I hope you understand."

Barton, simply, replies, "They are pretty sorry friends to let you die for that."

Bang!

Wayne is sitting in the saddle, blood pouring from the center of his chest as he struggles to get his gun free from its leather pocket. Barton pulls the hammer back on his Colt sidearm, ready to finish off his assailant before he can get off a desperate effort. But there will be no second shot needed, as Wayne slowly slides off the left side of his mount, his body lifeless before it hits the ground.

"Pick your friend up, put him across his horse, and get out of here. I really don't want to waste another bullet on anyone else, today."

Once they secure their friend's dead body across the saddle, Frank turns to Barton, with a worried look on his face, and inquires, "You know that all that hogwash talking and taking you on was his idea, right? We wanted no part of this. We aren't going to have to worry about you coming after us like you did Angus Ford, are we? You can forget this happened, right?"

Barton, staying cool and calm, answers, "You just better be glad the big gray horse wasn't here, he doesn't forget anything!"

As Barton watches the strangers leave, Swift Eagle rides up beside him. In his manner of being to the point, the young chief shares an observation that has been growing since the two first met, many days ago at the stone field fence.

"Anderson, you are not one to waste a lot of words negotiating your way out of hostile situations, are you?"

Barton, continuing to make sure the obtruders do not have a change of heart and return, lays his hand upon his holstered pistol and answers, "Mr. Colt says it a lot better than I can."

Swift Eagle and White Bear let out war whoops of approval at their tall friend's response and attitude.

It is evening when the weary travelers make their way into the Shawnee encampment. The tribe had been made aware of their emergent chief's return when braves, who had been riding sentry patrols, observed the foursome while still some distance away. Upon hearing the pronouncements of the sentries, the natives start preparing for a festive meal and a traditional celebration when the victorious warriors return to camp. Swift Eagle is greeted with charismatic shouts, animated hand gestures, and freestyle dancing. But the loudest response was when the proud father lifted his son high in the air, for all to see that the future chief, of the High Plains Shawnee nation, was well and had returned.

"Little Hawk! Grandson of the mighty warrior Red Hawk! Son of our great chief, Swift Eagle," were the shouts that filled the air, in their native language and impromptu songs.

Barton, quietly, sits and watches the festivities, out of the line of recognition. He felt that this was an important part of the bonding of the Shawnee people with their new tribal leader. But his anonymity would not be long-lived, as Swift Eagle begins shouting and pointing to him. The louder, and the more, that Swift Eagle cries out, the more intense the throng of natives focus their attention his way. Then, almost in unison, they start speaking one name. Their vocalization starts in a low volume but grows louder with each expression.

"Judeahay! Judeahay! Judeahay!"

Soon, the entire throng of Shawnee celebrators are surrounding the apprehensive cowboy, who is still sitting upon a growingly nervous Jake. Suddenly, the chanting, the drum beating, and the dancing stopped. Without provocation or coercion, an opening appears in the tribal circle that has surrounded the tall man on the buckskin horse. Swift Eagle, now feeling more confident in his position among his people, rides up to the side of Barton, extends his arm toward his respected friend. When Barton returns the offering, Swift Eagle grabs his forearm and proclaims...

"Tonight, the High Plains Shawnee are feeling the favor of the Great Fathers, our spirits are high, and our native pride rises again. We shall make our campfires dance, we shall share the venison and the bounty of our gardens, and we shall welcome a new brother to the Shawnee circle. Tonight, we shall sit, eat, and parlay with the great Shadow Warrior, Judeahay!"

As the passionate chanting, dancing, and rhythmic drum beating resumes, the young chief looks at his new white friend, and with a gesture that might suggest that the man with the Henry rifle could be rubbing off on his young native ally, Swift Eagle smiles and then winks.

Barton, shaking his head in amazement for the moment, replies, "Good enough!"

Once the official social soiree commences, it is quite the shindig. Barton is given a place of honor next to Swift Eagle. Large chunks of venison, fresh off of the roaring firepit, are passed around the growing circle of participants. Cobs of roasted corn follow, and soon baskets of varied berries, are picked by the women of the tribe. Barton could not remember the last time that he had shared a moment with so many people, with so much goodwill and spirit. Probably, he thought as he cut another piece of venison off, it would be one of the church socials in Smithview. His mind, for a moment, saw an image of Jenny standing at the stove, waiting for her pies to finally finish baking. But Barton would not linger upon that picture, for he knew the intense sorrow that would soon follow.

At some point, Barton notices that the abundant flow of food starts to slow down. Then, Swift Eagle is handed a long, leather bag. Upon opening it, the leader of the Shawnee people removes an ornately carved, wooden pipe. He dips the pipe into another bag, careful not to spill any of the contents that have been dipped into the bowl. Once he has spoken an intense Shawnee decree, to those who are respectfully anticipating the next part of the evening, Swift Eagle pulls a flaming chard, out of the fire, and touches it to the bowl on the pipe. With two long puffs, the tribal leader hands the pipe to Barton.

Realizing that every eye is now upon him, and he needs to be careful not to insult the traditions of these proud people, he starts to take a draw from the long, oaken smoking device. Just as he takes a big breath, a strange thought rushes to his mind, 'this smells a lot like the mossy substance that the braves used when treating Smoke'. If it is, then Barton is pretty certain how this evening is going to, eventually, conclude. For a second, he fights between the decision to participate or to play it safe and pass it on. One look at the awaiting Swift Eagle solicits the only response that Barton can give on this jubilant night...

"Oh, what the hell!"

The actual events of the remaining evening will be a little hazy from this point. Barton will remember that there were a lot of loud voices, chanting and dancing, storytelling that seemed to grow in exaggeration as the ceremonial pipe made its rounds, and the continued uttering of the phrase 'Judeahay'. While the attention, and the constant staring at him, is difficult for him to handle, Barton figures that it is important to his hosts to have him there. Swift Eagle, in particular, seemed to draw a sense of satisfaction to have the Shadow Warrior sitting at his side. For the night, Barton will be resolved to let the Shawnee have their moment and their celebration. If his being there added to the level of fulfillment, then 'pass the pipe' and let this evening be one to remember for all.

At some point, with the fervor of the ceremonies ebbing, Barton searches for a secluded place to lie down and process what has just happened. Taking the colorful blanket that someone has placed around him, at some unknown point in the festivities, he finds a spot that will offer solitude and fireside warmth. As he settles his long frame in a comfortable posture, his mind wanders from realities to dreams. At one moment in time, he senses that someone has positioned themselves beside him. He isn't sure of the identity of this mystery person, but he ventures that it is a young Shawnee maid. He can feel her gentle hand touching his face. The sensation of her warm breath stirs memories of when he and Jenny would sit next to the fireplace at the ranch house. Barton struggles to gather his consciousness. He needs to explain that his heart is still loyal to the memory of his precious wife. But, upon opening his eyes to start his soliloquy of appreciation for the attention, Barton is surprised by the sight before him...two large nostrils enveloped within a dark gray muzzle.

"Oh, Smoke! I should have known it was you, my old amigo."

The great horse whinnies and shuffles his front hooves, clearly pleased with the reaction of his traveling partner.

Barton encourages his equine friend to get some rest, for the morning is coming and they have many miles yet to travel.

18

The Kansas horizon seems to come to life as the morning sun makes its appearance. Barton has said his goodbyes to Swift Eagle, saddled up Jake, and is well into the three-hour ride to the Givens' ranch. Smoke is trotting around Barton, still not used to seeing his traveling companion upon another animal. The big gray stallion, occasionally, challenges Jake by running at the buckskin, slapping his front hooves against the ground and making that high-pitched sound that signals that Smoke is 'on the scene' and ready for action.

"I told you this is just a temporary arrangement," Barton says. "You are not ready to carry a rider any distance, yet. You haven't been replaced, so quit acting like you are some kind of expelled royalty. I think you let the Shawnee fill your head with a lot of that 'Tonkakee' nonsense. Well, old boy, starting today, Judeahay and Tonkakee have ridden off into the sunset, got it?"

Smoke shakes his head, in a rebellious manner. But, for the

remainder of the trip, he will be content with giving Jake an occasional stern look and surly snort.

It has been a while since Barton has been alone to process how things have played out the last three weeks. It started with catching up with Coy Newton and dispatching the last of those who took his family from him. At that time, Barton had no reason to live and was prepared for life to end, and did not care. But the surprising revelation that Seth was alive put something in his mind, and heart, that had been gone for a long time. While he still suffered from the loss of most positive emotions to face each day, Barton had a reason to move forward, and that was a major change in how things had been.

Upon becoming the state's 'proxy for back-alley justice', he had become a cold, calculating loner, so as to keep things simpler. But recent circumstances have opened doors for a patchwork of people to come into his life. In each one's specific way, they assisted in the multi-faceted search, and rescue, of his son. Farther Porter, Issac Mayes, Rand and Wilber, and Swift Eagle have shown that a person can allow outside assistance without surrendering control of one's life. Barton knows that others will need to be integrated into what will be a different routine with Seth at the center of it. For so long, Barton thought of nothing other than going about his responsibilities as 'the janitor'. And while that commitment will have to be managed and maintained, Barton is easing into the thought that being a father and a covert agent for justice can co-exist. Yes, it's going to take a lot of work and preparation, but the rewards are going to be worth it. And the thought of something being 'worth it' is, definitely, going to take some time to ease into.

As he rides along, Barton reflects on how the last three weeks have unfolded. First, he finds out that Seth is alive. Then, he learns that his son has been sold to the highest bidder, like a spring calf. Next, upon finding where Seth is, he gets seriously hurt trying to get his son back, unexpectedly gets his son back, and faces a paid lunatic gunman to keep his son. To add to the unfolding drama, he nearly has to put down his horse after Smoke was shot by the gunman. Barton's thoughts become forlorn as he thinks of how a tribe of people had to pay a dear price because they helped him escape the reprisal of a rich, evil man. Through it all, Barton is amazed at how it culminates with the carrying out of a daring extrication of the son of a Shawnee chief while killing the rich man and the hired gun. A lot to experience in a very short time. So, now, it is time to reunite with his son and return to Smithview to set up a new life with the youngest Anderson.

The first contact that Barton makes, upon riding upon the Given's spread, is a group of ranch workers who are driving a sizable herd of Herefords closer to the main house. With winter just a few weeks away, it will be easier to manage the livestock during the harder season. Verbal greetings and hand gestures meet Barton, as his presence is noticed by the cowboys. In a matter of minutes, one rider comes racing up to where Barton, Smoke, and Jake are moseying around the five-hundred head of prized beef.

"Hey, big man! So glad to see you back. I am sure there is a kid who is going to be pretty excited to have his dad back with us!"

Barton tips his hat at the salutation from Carl, the ranch foreman. When Carl rides up beside Barton, they automatically extend their hands and share a hearty greeting. Not to be left out, Smoke trots up to the lead ranch hand, extends his chin out, and waits for the obligatory rub of acknowledgment.

"Yes, big gray, it is good to see you too! Looks like he is recovering well from the gunshot wound, Anderson!"

Barton nods his head, in agreement, and inquires how things are at the main house. Carl shares that Asa has been a new man, with a seven-year-old around the ranch. The ranch owner has desired to have kids around the place to fuss over, and Seth has been the apple of the old man's eye ever since Barton left. Everyone has taken to the youngest Anderson and, it seems, that Seth has grown accustomed to life at the big house. Carl, even, shares that if Given gets his wish, Barton will not make plans to leave, but will choose to make the ranch his home, too.

Barton, slowly, shakes his head and replies, "I see there have been a lot of things going on, things that I should be grateful for. But, we have a life waiting for us, in Smithview, and a family for the boy to get to know."

Carl, in an attempt to prepare Barton, says, "I am just telling you, the old man isn't going to give up easy on convincing you to change your address. It's going to be hard for him to say goodbye to the boy, especially."

"I appreciate what you are telling me, but I haven't even had the luxury of spending the quality time, with Seth, that you folks have. I need to find out who this kid is, and let him know who his father is," Barton states, with a sense of anticipation in his voice.

By noontime, Barton can see the main structures of the Givens' operation. Upon closer examination, as he gets closer, he can see a single horse running toward him. It is clear that it is Asa Givens. At first, Barton surmises that the old cowboy is alone, but a youthful voice soon reveals that that is not the case.

"Daddy! It's really you, Daddy!"

Seth is not noticeable, at first, because he is riding behind the elder rancher, clinching his young arms around Givens and hanging on for all he can. But, before Givens can pull his mount beside Barton, Seth stands up and jumps from one horse to the other without coming to a complete stop. Barton, not used to being assailed in such a manner, barely catches Seth as he grabs his father around the neck, implementing an embrace that takes Barton's breath away.

"Hey boy, good to see you too! But, if you don't want me to pass out and fall off, you better loosen your grip, just a bit. I think someone else is glad to see you, too. You glad to see your old friend, Smoke?"

Before Barton can explain that the big gray equine is still recovering from his wound, Seth has sprung from Jake to the awaiting Smoke. Sitting firmly astride the great horse, Seth lays his head down on Smoke's neck, places his arms down on each side of the stallion's neck, and proceeds to show his appreciation for the appearance of his four-legged friend. Even though he does not have any riding tack on, Smoke will take all care in protecting his young rider, as they head back to the big ranch house.

"So good to see you, cowboy!" Givens shares. "The boy has looked, every day, hoping to see you and that horse coming across the prairie. Today is a great day! We will celebrate and welcome you back with the best meal the house staff can prepare, plenty of Kentucky bourbon and Tijuana cigars, and listen as you tell the whole story of how you made those bastards sorry they ever messed with the man with the Henry rifle!"

Barton, wearily, chuckles and shares that if an extended time of peace and quiet would not be perceived as being rude, he is willing to wait on the great party and celebration.

The ranch owner nods his head, in the affirmative, and says, "Sir, I understand. I am sure that it has been a hard journey and mission. You tell us when you are ready to 'knock back a few', smoke a long one, and chow down on some of the best BBQ this side of heaven. Until then, you won't know there is a soul in the place. That is my promise."

Barton, knowing that ranch life is not a place where total

tranquility can be expected, appreciates the gesture and salutes his host with a touch of the brim of his cowboy hat.

Once he did locate a bed, in the large ranch house, it would be twelve hours before Barton would show his face to an anticipating boy, an awaiting host, and a house staff ready to see to his every desire. The sleep was deep and resting, despite the usual ranch life proceeding around him. Upon arising from the large feather mattress, Barton finds that his clothes have been laundered, his boots cleaned, and a new Stetson hat has replaced the old, worn headgear that Barton has worn for a few years. Even his guns, both the Henry and Colt, were looking shinier, operating smoother, and had the smell of fresh gun oil upon them. While, for a short moment, Barton thought that a man could get used to such amenities, he cleared his mind of such considerations as he knew that his life was best served simple and to the point. But, for now, he will be sure to tell the elder rancher that the gestures were appreciated.

While enjoying a stove-cooked meal, the first in a while, Barton has the challenge of listening to two different conversation wellsprings simultaneously. On his left, Seth is updating his dad on every single event the boy has experienced since Barton had left to rescue Little Hawk. To the right, a hopeful rancher explains how it would be better for Barton and Seth to live on the Givens spread. Barton could continue to do his work as a righteous vigilante, or whatever it was that Barton does, while Seth would be safely sheltered at a location that offered the protection of 30-40 armed cowboys. Givens spoke of bringing in tutors and teachers to ensure the youngster's education, the female house staff could nurture him in life and relationship matters, and Barton would still be the father that a young boy needs growing up. Barton could tell that Givens had given a lot of thought to this, and had even practiced his presentation beforehand.

As for Seth's storytelling, Barton just nodded and added a well-placed 'really' or 'that's good' to give the boy a sense that his reports were appreciated. The old rancher, though, was another matter. For now, Barton will not quench Asa's dreams of his visitors becoming permanent residents at the cattle spread. If it meant this much for Givens to put so much effort in how to explain why it should happen, Barton figures that he should take as much time to find the words to explain why it could not happen.

For the next three days, it will be a time for continued healing, hoping, and herding. Barton could see that Smoke was running more fluidly and with more stamina. Even the spirited contrariness was back in the big gray's eyes and actions. The rest, good food, and positive interactions had benefited both horse and rider, as Barton could feel the improvement in his physical status. Givens still spoke of the Andersons taking up residence, on the ranch, but he could see that he was losing the battle, as Barton and Seth would often talk of what it would be like to be back in Smithview. Toward the end of their stay at the engaging livestock operation, Barton and Smoke spent time helping with moving cattle herds and cutting calves to be shipped to market. It had been a long time since Barton had done ranch work, and while the instincts were still there, the heart to do it was gone. There will always be a void of desire without Jenny to share in the dream.

When the day to leave finally came, there was a somber mood that filled the air. During breakfast, Asa tried to convince Barton of the advantages of living there. And while he could not argue with the elder statesman's valid points, Barton explained that friendship and devotion could not take the place of family and the love that comes with it. To make sure that Barton would return, the old rancher told Barton to use Jake to get back to Smithview. For one thing, Smoke was not quite ready to carry

Barton and Seth, and the other motive was to give Barton a reason to come back to return the big buckskin, someday. Barton shook Givens' hand and assured him that he would be back, maybe in the spring when the fish were jumping out of the running streams and the elk were out for the mating season. Asa smiled and said that he would look forward to that, and seeing his young friend again.

When he had completed checking the saddle bags, belly cinches, and bridle straps, Barton placed Seth upon Smoke and then mounted upon the awaiting Jake. Barton figured that having Seth travel on Smoke would be wise for two reasons; Seth would be a lighter load for the big gray horse to carry, and Smoke would be more careful transporting his little buddy, whom the stallion had known from the time Seth was born.

"If you are ever through here, looking for cutthroats and killers, you know you are always welcome to stop. A Cuban stogie and a glass of the good stuff will always be waiting," Givens shouts out, as the Anderson duo resume their journey to Smithview.

Both father and son seem to be in good spirits, this Kansas day. There is a sense that they are equipped, prepared, and ready for whatever challenges and experiences may be waiting for them. But they could never be ready for what will be coming, one day, in the not-so-distant future. Will life ever let the Anderson family go a length of time without having to have their very foundations shaken to within the breaking point? Will Barton ever be able to let his guns grow quiet, instead of hunting for the those whom he has been directed to purge from Kansas, forever?

The next 6 months will be a time of learning, renewing, and enjoying each other, for Barton and Seth. The reunion with Jeff, Sally, and the boys will go very well. Seth seems to enjoy having his bed back, in the loft. Jeff and Sally are making a point to watch Seth, to not let the past things weigh heavy upon his young heart and mind. They try very hard never to position themselves as 'replacements' for Jenny and Adam, but just family that is there to help move forward. Barton can see that having the cousins is a favorable step in Seth's life. Enjoying someone to just be a 'boy' with, play ball, mumbly peg, or laying on one's back and looking at the clouds in the sky with, these have been missing in the young Anderson's life and are now back.

As for the aspect of having a father-son relationship that could only be experienced in portions of time, this is taking a little more effort and understanding. Smoke has his part down, immediately. Upon Barton giving the directive to retrieve Seth from the distant ranch, the obedient equine is very efficient in his order of business, which consists of announcing his arrival with a loud whinny, waiting for Seth to appear, standing for the young Anderson to climb aboard, and then, carefully at a smooth galloping pace, bringing the son to his awaiting father. Like clockwork would be the best way to describe this part of the Anderson life.

Barton is the one who seems to have to make the most adjustments at having a seven-year-old around his subterranean hide-a-way. As for the accommodations, Seth finds it like going camping or spelunking. Sally has sent plenty of bedding and extra clothes and Jeff has built a special cedar chest for the personal items to be kept in, especially when Barton has to be away, and Seth is back at the ranch.

The cavern habitat is, surprisingly, turning out to be a very hospitable place to dwell in. When it was just Barton, there were not any needs for the comfort afforded by a more traditional structure. It offered a place that was cool in the summer, warm in the winter, and dry at all times, with the exception of a small spring that trickled down a wall, into a catch basin and over-flowed out a crevice to the exterior. When adding a second inhabitant, there is plenty of space to stretch out without feeling claustrophobic. Nature had provided a natural draft, through a network of fissures, fractures, and natural vents, that kept the air fresh, the campfire smoke vacated and mold from forming on the limestone walls. There is even enough space for Smoke to come in to get out of the elements. In the great horse's corner, Barton constructed a wooden structure where a saddle, bridle, and other tack could be kept off of the ground. Jeff, again, would make periodic trips to the natural hangout to refill an old pickle barrel with oats, corn, and a square, or two, of red clover hay. Seth takes it upon himself to keep Smoke's area cleaned out and ready for the return of the big gray one.

It wasn't the transportation or the housing, of Seth, that

presented a learning curve for Barton. It was brushing up on the ability to converse with a seven-year-old, especially when the talents of personal interaction have not been a priority for the lone gunman. One-word answers and short-sentenced observations will not be enough when passing time with a young boy. Seth, with the encouragement to chatter while with the ranch family, finds it odd to come to a situation where generous discourses are few and silent contemplation is more the rule for the day. Barton tries to engage his son in meaningful, resonant discussions, but the days of traveling alone are not breeding grounds for developing the 'gift of the gab'. The duo will, eventually, find a middle ground where they can meet and still value the time they spend together. The fact that they are together, again, is the greatest joy of this whole undertaking.

Another change has happened in Barton's life, and that deals with the procedure in how the 'janitor' duties are carried out. In the previous assignments, Marshal Tomes would ride to Smithview, and place a large portion of the reward funds into a special account designated for ranch expenses and the new costs of Seth living there, now. The remainder of the recompense, for Barton's completion of dealing with heinous outlaws, the marshal would bring to the Rooster Pass den where he would give it to Barton, along with his next engagement. From time to time, Tomes would be involved with matters, in another part of the state, and he would send Jason Nash with the expense money and the new directive. But, it has been a while since the marshal has visited with Barton, sending Jason the last three times. Barton figures that two things may be a factor in the marshal's absence, the duties of a federal lawman or the growing obligations of a burgeoning relationship with Nurse Baird, in Prestonburg. Barton smirked at the thought of his friend having to tow in the privileges of bachelorhood for the expectations of a woman's attention. He is sure that the latter was the reason Tomes was not making it to Smithview, as often.

It is April, spring is starting to come to life in Kansas, when Barton returns, to Rooster Pass from another productive exercise in clandestine justice. Smoke, upon arriving at the mountain lair, drops off his tall rider and heads to the ranch to get Seth. Barton is amazed at how this part of his life has gone from 'awkward' to 'authentic' and how he can trade the 'janitor' persona for that of 'faithful father' without missing a beat. With the improved weather comes more things for him to do with his growing son. Now eight years old, Barton sees Seth changing, both physically and intellectually. At times, Barton will misspeak and call him 'Adam' because the youngest Anderson is approaching that place in life where Adam was. Seth just shrugs his shoulders and never embarrasses his dad by pointing out the mistake. After realizing his error, Barton catches a glimpse of Jenny in Seth's sense of mercy and forgiveness for this father's blunders, just as Jenny would never correct someone, especially if it came at the cost of that person's dignity.

The periodic reunions between father and son are scenes that start with Seth telling of all his adventures while Barton was away. Barton is, now, able to get involved in the conversation by asking timely questions and sharing exclamations of awe at the splendidness of each account. Next, the paternal duo will turn their attention to Smoke, Barton attends to the removal and storing of all tack, while Seth gives the mighty horse a thorough brushing, enlightening Smoke with a repeat of the stories that he just imparted to his father. Smoke gives the young Anderson his undivided attention, with an occasional nicker to encourage the young storyteller. Next will come the preparations for a meal, prepared over a fire that will be started in the cave's ash pit. Barton, when he can, will bring home something that he has shot along the way, either a rabbit, squirrel, or prairie chicken. If there were no chances to secure the game for supper, Sally keeps Seth's cedar chest stocked with cans of beans, cold-packed meat, and peaches. Tonight, the Anderson men will feast on rabbit, pan-fried potatoes, and a can of sweet Colorado peaches.

It was in the midst of what Seth referred to as 'the time to be quiet and think', after a supper meal, that the evening would have a dreadful change in mood. It started with Smoke slapping his feet onto the ground and making that low, growling sound that usually precedes an unexpected appearance of a friend or stranger.

"Daddy, what is wrong with Smoke? Something seems to have him upset."

Barton, raising his tall frame from the reclining position that he had taken after eating, replies, "It usually means that someone is coming, or they are here, unannounced. You stay here while I go outside to see which is the case."

Upon walking outside the stoney abode, he surveys in every direction, eventually observing what looks like a rider coming from the direction of Smithview. Despite being told to wait inside, Seth joins his father in watching the approaching horseman.

"They are riding pretty hard, daddy. Do you think it is Marshal Tomes? Maybe he has a problem and needs you to help him, "remarks Seth.

Barton, rubbing his unshaven jaw, shakes his head to the negative and answers, "It's not Tomes, for that is not Hickory under that rider. That horse is smaller and lighter in color. If I didn't know better, I would say it is Jason Nash. But I can't imagine why he would be riding 'hell for leather' at this time of night."

Barton's guess turns out to be true, for it is Jason Nash, riding a bay pony that is covered with lather from a prolonged, hard ride from town.

"Mr. Anderson......Mr. Anderson," the young gunsmith yells, as he tries to get a breath in between his attempts to announce his arrival.

"Son, slow down, take a big breath, and gather yourself," Barton exclaims as he grabs the rein of the bay horse, in an attempt to find out what this is all about.

Jason gets off of his horse, bends over while placing his hands on his knees, and struggles for any fresh air to enter his exhausted lungs. Once he stands up, the cheerless look on the young man's face tells Barton this is not going to be good news. Jason, without saying a word, hands Barton what looks like a telegram. After reading what is in the wire dispatch, Barton slaps his hands together and lets loose with a one-word reaction.

"Damn!"

"What is going on, Daddy? What does it say? Jason, why did Daddy say that?"

Jason, at this point, is not fighting for a breath, anymore. Now, he is fighting back tears.

Even though Barton is not saying anything, Seth knows this is not a good dispatch. The way his father is standing, and staring off into the distance, is a posture the young Anderson has seen before when Barton is fighting old feelings that are rising inside him.

"Jason, when you get yourself collected, take Seth back to the ranch," was all Barton will share as he goes into the cave, saddles up Smoke, and tears out in a northern direction. Seth, still confused and unaware of the situation, reaches down to pick up the telegram that Barton dropped after reading it. Seth gasps upon reading its contents...

MARSHAL TOMES SHOT IN PRESTONBURG(STOP) COME ASAP(STOP) PROGNOSIS DIRE (STOP)

Barton and Smoke will ride hard all night and into the morning. The full moon, over the Kansas countryside, makes travel easier. The night sky, the pace of the journey, and the tenor of the reason for it reminds Barton of another night when he was attempting to get to his family before tragedy did. All he can do is try, and hope, that he is more successful this time around.

Smoke was performing like the great steed that he is, legs and feet moving effortlessly and swiftly. Barton, conscious of the time since the stallion had been wounded, tries to get Smoke to pace himself. But this horse seems to have the ability to sense when his rider is at a heightened anxiety and feed off of that increased energy. Plus, maybe Smoke understood that the marshal was the big gray's chin-rubbing friend, too.

Prestonburg was well into the morning when the travelers arrived at Dr. Tilley's clinic. No sooner had Barton dismounted from Smoke than he heard the front door of the medical facility open. It was Nurse Baird. Barton was struck by how the usually attractive woman looked so tired, so fraught. Once he stepped upon the front porch, she laid her head upon his chest and wept uncontrollably.

"How is he doing?" was all that Barton could muster at the moment.

Stepping back a step and wiping the tears from her exhausted face, she answers, "The doctor says that he has done all he can do. Lyndon took a shot to the chest, point blank range. Doc says that may have given him any hope of surviving because the bullet was through him before it started coming apart. Mr. Anderson, he has been in a coma from the moment they got him here. He comes out of it, from time to time. When he does, he asks if you are here yet. I love him so much and I cannot bear the thought of losing him."

Barton places his hand on the back of his neck, which he

does when he is trying to make sense of a situation. He starts to go into the clinic, but turns back to the agonizing lady and enquires as to how this happened, how Tomes could have been caught so off-guard.

"We were at Granny Ryan's, our usual place to share a meal and a quiet moment. I think he was getting ready to propose, or he was acting like he was. But, out of nowhere, a young man walked up, introduced himself, placed the barrel of his pistol against Lyndon's badge, and fired his gun into his chest. No warning, nothing. Just 'I am Calvin Ford, and you shouldn't have stopped the big man'. What does that mean, Mr. Anderson?"

Barton closes his eyes and tilts his head back, absolutely stunned by this revelation. Barton will not add to Nurse Baird's heartache by revealing that this could all have been avoided. That is, if Barton had just fired his Henry rifle that day when the Ford clan faced off with him, and Tomes, on the way to Smithview.

"Doesn't matter now," Barton replied, as he placed his hand upon her back and escorted her back into the clinic.

Once inside, Barton is greeted by Dr. Tilley, who also looks like he has had a long, trying ordeal attempting to keep the federal lawman alive. The physician just shakes his head, in a manner that would suggest that the situation is bleak, and opens the door to where Tomes is set up. Barton positions himself beside the medical bed, taking a seat on an adjacent chair. For the next few minutes, Barton watches as his friend lays still, breathing in short, shallow respirations. Barton has never seen this strong man look so vulnerable, so helpless. But, without remembering, it was in this very room that the tall man had laid, much in the same condition, and Tomes was the one sitting beside the bed, wondering if the next breath would be the last.

It wasn't long after Barton's arrival that Tomes opened his eyes, turned his head toward his friend sitting nearby, and smiled to let Barton know that the marshal was content to see him. Then, Tomes struggled to lift a clenched fist in the cowboy's direction. When Barton places his open hand underneath, the marshal relaxes his grip and drops something into Barton's hand. Upon examining the item, Barton is hit hard by the recognition of what it is...

Tomes' marshal badge, a gaping bullet hole in the middle of it, is still stained with the lawman's blood.

After looking up at the weeping woman, whom he had hoped to make his bride, Tomes focuses back on Barton, who sees that his friend is struggling to speak something that appears to be crucial for his cowboy friend to know. Barton leans forward to make it easier for Tomes to share this essential detail. Then, summoning up all the strength that he has left, the marshal speaks one word, but it says all that needs to be said, especially for Barton.

"Vindication!"

Barton takes Tomes' hand into his own, and responds, "Oh, hell yes! You can count on it!"

And, with that message shared between the two friends, Tomes takes one last, deep breath and closes his eyes for the last time.

"Oh, Lyndon! Don't leave me now," cried Nurse Baird, as she sits on the side of the bed and touches the face of her fallen darling and beau.

She will still be, softly, stroking Tomes' face when Barton gets up and leaves the room. Upon walking outside, he heads to Smoke, who seems to sense that this is a moment when his travel friend will need him. Barton takes the great horse by the chin, rubbing the soft appendage as he has done so many times before. Barton, with that feeling of retributive justice swelling within him, stands and stares at the Henry rifle upon Smoke's saddle. He never hears her walk up to him, but he hears the words that the devastated lady whispers to him.

"I don't know who Calvin Ford is, I don't know how he ever came into Lyndon's life. Right now, I don't really care. All I know is that I waited my whole life for a man like Lyndon Tomes to walk into it, to love me for who I am, and to want to spend the rest of his life with me. For a moment, I had it all. And now, thanks to a violent stranger walking up and playing God with a man's life, I have nothing. Nothing, Mr. Anderson, but heartache and a sense of total emptiness. I know one thing, I do not ever want to have to sit in a courtroom and have to hear how my future husband's killer was just a misunderstood young man and can be rehabilitated if given the chance. Do you understand me, Mr. Anderson? Do you understand what I am asking of you?"

Barton gets upon Smoke, leans over toward Nurse Baird, and answers.

"I promise, very soon, Calvin Ford will be burning in hell!"

And with that said, Barton sets out to find the killer of Marshal Lyndon Tomes.

THE END, for now...

ABOUT THE AUTHOR

GK Beatty's life has not been boring. From a small town Kentucky farmboy, to a well-known radio personality, then becoming a Baptist minister, and now a published author.

Thru it all, one thing was common to each stop in the highway - writing. While the subject focus changed, upon arrival at each destination, the talent was always there to express what was going on in the "theatre of the mind".

Now, GK gets to live the dream, relive the memories and write about one of his greatest loves, the American Western. As he often states, "life is still good!"

ALSO BY GK BEATTY

The Vindicated Man (Barton Anderson Book One)

Millions of people love *Yellowstone*, loved *Lonesome Dove*, and will love 'The Vindicated Man'. The spirit of the American West is still alive and still captures the imaginations, and hearts, of those who travel there. Thru the theatre of the mind and dreams of a life lived long ago, '*The Vindicated Man*' will prove that it continues to be lived today.

Barton Anderson was setting on top of the world, he had a life most men could only dream of. Then, in just a matter of hours, it was all taken from him. Life will never be the same. Barton Anderson will never be the same. Those who come in contact with him will never be the same. When you have nothing to lose, and vengeance is all you want, the journey is very simple, but vindication may be impossible to find.

Following in the best traditions of Louis L'Amour, Zane Grey and JT Edson, GK Beatty has brought back the moral certainty of America's historic Wild West, where true grit and hope could win the day and triumph over evil. You can relive these tough yet exciting times in '*The Vindicated Man*'.

What the readers say about The Vindicated Man:

'I have read a lot of westerns, this one ranks as one of the top 10.'

'I liked the entire book from start to finish, once started couldn't put it down.'

'I was captivated from page one!'

'I read the book in two days. I couldn't put it down.'